"IT IS A TIME OF GREAT DANGER. AND THE DANGER IS FROM YOUR VESSEL."

"Where is my ship?" the alien girl asked suddenly. "What has been done with the *Death?"*

"Nothing has been done with it," I said, with sinking heart. "And we hoped that you would know where it is and how it can be stopped. Is it possible you don't know what the *Death's* mission was?"

The girl's face darkened. "The mission was to kill."

"That, I know. I saw what your weapons did to the Delphinus sun."

"The *Death* is functioning?"

"Too well. It attacked Sigma Libra. There was a Fleet outpost on an outermost Sigma planet. It is vapor now." Now it was her turn to feel my emotions, and they were laced with anger, bitterness, and frustration. I had been so certain that the girl would be the key to unlock the mystery of the murderous starship, and now I was unsure . . .

Ace Science Fiction books by Robert Cham Gilman

THE WARLOCK OF RHADA
THE REBEL OF RHADA
THE NAVIGATOR OF RHADA
THE STARKAHN OF RHADA

ROBERT CHAM GILMAN

THE STARKAHN OF RHADA

ACE SCIENCE FICTION BOOKS
NEW YORK

This Ace Science Fiction Book
contains the complete text of the original
hardcover edition. It has been completely
reset in a typeface designed for easy
reading, and was printed from new film.

THE STARKAHN OF RHADA

An Ace Science Fiction Book/published by arrangement with
the author

PRINTING HISTORY
Harcourt, Brace & World edition published 1970
Ace Science Fiction edition/June 1986

ISBN: 0-441-78205-1

Ace Science Fiction Books are published by The Berkley Publishing Group,
200 Madison Avenue, New York, New York 10016.
PRINTED IN THE UNITED STATES OF AMERICA

For C. F. C. and Sam

THE STARKAHN OF RHADA

Prologue

In the beginning was Earth, and Earth's First Stellar Empire. Before the First Empire were ten thousand years of man's yearning to reach the stars.

For a few short decades in the heart of that beginning, man reached farther still, beyond the galaxy, to the Lesser Magellanic Cloud. This was Transportation, the Long Death—the voyage had many names. An expanding society cast out its misfits and criminals: cast them beyond the Rim of the main galaxy and into oblivion.

In time, gentler methods were found to deal with society's unwanted, and men no longer died the Long Death. And there came wars and times of trouble; the First Empire struggled to survive and did not. The transportees were long forgotten.

The First Empire died in fire and blood, and there was the Interregnum—the Dark Age. Nyor, queen city of the skies, became a village, a ruin, and then, in the fullness of time, a town, a city, a capital once again. On the brow of Tel-Manhat, between the two rivers, Nyor ruled a planet, then a solar system, and, finally, the Second Stellar Empire. And her vessels, crewed by men of a thousand client nations, again roamed the galaxy. Such is the cyclic nature of history.

But wherever man's seed has been planted—there, too, is history. And endeavor. And *purpose* . . .

The great black ship orbited the white dwarf star at a distance of one hundred ninety-seven million kilometers in this, its eight thousandth winter season: a starship unlike any seen by men of the main galaxy since time out of mind. Larger than a small planetoid, its great size humbled even the ancient starships of the First Empire. Yet it strangely resembled them. From blunt nose to oddly flattened tail, it measured seventeen kilometers; in diameter, something over five. The light of the blue-white star was deadened by the dull black metal. The immense craft had a sullen, menacing look to it. Peculiarly formed antennae and projections hinted at an inhuman technology, a perverse and hostile science.

The ship spun slowly. Once in each forty-three Earth Standard Hours it exposed the totality of its billion metric tons to the glare of the distant, deadly star. Once in eighty-four years, it circled its primary. It had orbited here (around a star so obscure it had no name, only a number) in the densely starred galactic center almost one hundred times since it had first appeared in the nebular mist during a violent plasma storm.

Seen from a distance of a dozen kilometers, the huge hull would blot out a quarter of the blazing, starry sky. The metal of its flanks was pitted and scarred by the impact of billions upon billions of tiny particles and dust motes. The distance it had traveled was near to meaningless when expressed in kilometers. It had completed its journey while the Galactons of the time men still called the Golden Age ruled a million worlds. Helpless, it had waited through the Dark Time, through the centuries of the Second Empire's infancy, through the new Renaissance and the Age of Enlightenment, unable to awaken the single being within its gargantuan hull.

Inside, all was darkness. The generators and sensors and servo-control mechanisms of the ship's violent weapons systems were intact. They were superb devices, for all the technology of an embittered civilization had gone into their construction. More than thirty variations of solar-phoenix disruptors had been incorporated into the great black vessel's offensive power. Any one of a hundred weapons on board could destroy a star, many stars.

But to activate the ship, the builders had decreed that organic life must be aboard and conscious. The brain waves of a living human being were the keys unlocking Armageddon.

And the immense ship could not perform the simple task of awakening the being who lay in death sleep, preserved from time in a life-support capsule. Somewhere on its long, long voyage between the galaxies, the ship's primitive brain had been damaged. It was an engine of total, absolute war: the most vicious engine of destruction ever conceived by the mind of man. Still, no machine is proof against the hazards of the cosmos. Somewhere, millennia earlier and in the intergalactic deeps, a storm of radiation had scrambled the circuitry of the vessel's protonic brain. The computer signals intended to awaken the starship's single occupant on arrival had never been given.

Undiscovered, the great black starship might sleep forever.

So it swung in its lonely orbit around the white dwarf star that, in time, men came to discover through telescopes and to which they gave the name Delphinus 2380. Within the massive hull lay a single *Homo Magellansis:* almost human, not living, not dead.

Until—

Chapter One

Rhada, as we all know, is a nation of planets on the Rim of the galaxy. It produces brave men. Not always wise, mark you, but courageous. That is why I have made it my business to insure that the Rhad shall always be faithful to the Empire.

Attributed to Glamiss the Magnificent,
first Galacton of the Second Stellar Empire,
after the Battle of Karma

The Rhad are the bane of historians and the delight of generals, for they are the most foolhardy of men.

Mattias ben Mullerium,
The History of the Rhadan Republic,
late Second Stellar Empire period

I discovered it. So, being a Rhadan, I naturally found myself about to take a typically Rhadan plunge into the unknown. The specter of a Court of Inquiry nagged at my well-schooled military mind, but the ghosts of a hundred generations of warmen and princes said, "Go on!"

I stood at the lip of a dark pit, an open shaft in the flank of a starship so vast and so forbidding that it made my presence aboard dreamlike, nightmarish.

The shaft was black—blacker, even, than the dark metal of the monster vessel. The darkness swallowed the feeble beam of my light. I had the heart-squeezing notion that the blackness extended on through the ship to infinity, that if I committed myself to free fall and started down, I might plunge through the fabric of the familiar universe and through some terrifying star gate into another time, another dimension.

I realized, standing there in my space armor, the very picture of a soldier of the Empire, that I was not the stuff of which heroes are made. Heroes, I had always been led to believe, were men without fear: giants of character and intrepidity. My ancestors were like that: Kier, the Rebel of Rhada, for whom I was named, could never have known this gut-freezing fear. Surely not?

Yet here I was, formidable in armor, standing in open space on the flank of the most frightening derelict I had ever encountered in all my service with the Fleet.

My only contact with the familiar world of the Empire was Ariane. I could see her, a manta-shaped ADSPS cyborg, floating a kilometer or so distant, outlined against the glowing plasmas of the galactic center. It was all I could do to refrain from jetting to her and admitting that she had been right in disapproving my foolhardy decision to invade the mysterious great derelict alone. I could feel her concern flowing past the emotion-suppressing circuitry of the encephalophone.

Ariane, named for a queen, often behaved like one. An Armed Deep Space Probe Ship cyborg, she was a Fleet officer like myself and a full citizen of the Empire. As great as the ancients of the First Empire might have been, they never built anything to compare with Ariane and her fellow cyborgs of the Imperial Fleet's Survey Wing. The rest of the Empire's forces flew, at that time, the cumbersome antiques of the past: ships, not living beings. But the Survey Wing officers flew in company with ADSPS cyborgs, which even antiquarians must admit are the pinnacle of human space-technology.

Ariane said sharply, "What's happening?"

Ariane was receiving all my biosensor transmissions, of course, so she knew as well as I what was happening. (At the moment, all that was taking place was that I was nerving myself for the next step—over the edge of the shaft into the derelict.) But she was a *female* cyborg and liked to be told.

"I'm getting ready," I said subvocally into the E-phone.

"Your heart rate is up," the cyborg informed me mercilessly.

"I shouldn't be surprised."

"Standing by," she said. "Be careful."

The homey admonition was warming but hardly necessary. At my feet lay what seemed to be all the darkness in the universe. The slow rotation of the derelict gave me a slight negative gravity. I felt as though I might break free of my tenuous magnetic grip on the slope of the great metal planetoid and float out into the glowing plasma. Even this seemed preferable to plunging ahead into the black heart of the shaft, no matter what the shades of my noble ancestors urged me to do.

The white light of the Delphinus star glinted on Ariane's polished surfaces. She seemed to symbolize all safety and comfort, all the warmth of the loved and familiar. There was no ducking it: I was terrified. Training and heredity prevented me from crying out in fear, but that was all.

And I had come here—alone—at my own choice, against Ariane's recommendations, against Fleet regulations, and I had no one to blame but myself. I had left no options. I must go forward, or rather "down," into that Stygian darkness where there was no "down," no "up," no reference of any sort. And far worse, somewhere, in the miles of metal beneath my feet, a life-support system was functioning, keeping alive—what?

The price of heroics can be high for a dedicated nonhero. But I was a Rhad. In fact, I was the most Rhad of the Rhad, the Rhad Starkahn. In an earlier age, I would have been a king. The *need* to be courageous was upon me, for good or ill.

"I feel a bit disoriented," I said. It was my first extra-vehicular activity in space for months.

"Take a gravigen," Ariane ordered.

I activated my feeder and swallowed the bitter-tasting pill dry. It stuck in my throat. I shifted my weight and had to burn a thruster to hold myself in place on the metal landscape.

"Easy," cautioned Ariane. "There is an antenna array behind you. I think they are inert, but the Star knows what sort of radiation they emit. Stay clear of them."

"I'd better start down," I said hoarsely.

"Look around a bit first." The cyborg was as apprehensive as I, that was obvious. My heart overflowed with gratitude and affection for her.

I said, "No. I'd better do it now." I didn't finish the thought: *Or I won't do it all.*

The star was a brilliant arc light on the near black horizon. I took one last look at Ariane. She had just launched a message drone. The tiny, light-swift missile was gone, carrying copies of our tapes—just in case something prevented our return to a Fleet base. Sensible, but not very reassuring. I moved to the edge of the pit, sat down carefully. My booted feet hung over—what?

I gave a nervous laugh. "No point in loitering about, is there?" I imagined unspeakable things lurking down there in the iron belly of the derelict. Then training and discipline came to my aid, and I drew a deep breath. "I'm going," I called.

"Carefully," Ariane whispered.

"Rely on it," I said. I took one last look at the bright stars strewn thickly across the sky and stepped over the edge. I burned a thruster for direction, and the coaming swallowed the stars. I began to fall...

Only short hours before, Ariane and I had been routinely quartering the final segment of our patrol area. I had been sloughing off on my work, letting the cyborg do both the searching and cataloging. The large personal hoard of history tapes and films aboard were often my undoing, for I was, at that time, a bookish young man and as the noble Lady Nora Veg-Rhad (my mother) often said, inattentive to duty.

For several hours I had been deeply engrossed in Nav Julianus Mullerium's tape, *Anticlericalism in the Age of the Star Kings*, and when I get involved in that particular segment of the Empire's past, I lose track of time and almost everything else. It was Mullerium's account of some doings of my ancestor St. Emeric of Rhada that had me spellbound. But it was Ariane's almost miraculous competence that permitted me to be "inattentive."

No two ADSPS cyborgs are the same. Ariane is purely feminine—though sex isn't the same for a fifteen-metricton cyborg as it would be for a merely human woman. The psycho-medics who teamed Ariane and me must have known my mother. Certainly Ariane is every bit as strong-minded as Lady Nora. The medics must have thought I needed a mother figure to keep me in line while prowling the far reaches of the galaxy.

I admit I am bookish and perhaps overprotected. But I am still the Starkahn of Rhada, heir presumptive to the crown of a semiautonomous nation of twenty planets, including some rather well-populated ones, such as Gonlan and Aurora and Rhada itself. Of course there *is* no crown of Rhada any longer. The royalist Rhadan Palatinate became the very un-royalist Rhadan Republic two generations ago. Lady Nora, however, acts as though the new republicanism of our people were some sort of temporary mental lapse, a hiatus in the reign of the star kings. Her primary occupation seems to be encouraging rather pitiful little royalist plots against the "government of storekeepers," as she calls it.

I was trained in the profession of arms because the men of my family have always been so trained. Though Rhada has enjoyed varying degrees of independence and autonomy in the Second Stellar Empire, the ruling family of the Rhad has always served the Galacton, whoever he may be, who rules in Nyor on far-off Earth. For all of our independent airs, we have always been good Imperials and soldiers. But had I had any choice, I would have been a warlock, as learned men have been called since the Interregnum between the Empires. An historian, preferably; for that is where my interests have always been. My love of man's history through his millennia in space is great.

On this voyage Ariane and I had been charting stars in the densely starred region of the galactic center. Our operational area for the last sweep included the PPA, or Potential Planetary Area, of the stars Delphinus 2377 through 2382. These stars were all either white dwarfs or red giants and had produced only a few frozen methane planets with strong radiation belts. In addition to this, the nebulosity of the galactic center is pronounced, and the gas clouds and plasma storms tend to block translight commo systems. Consequently, we had been out of touch, peacefully so, with any Fleet base or commo beacon for two Earth Standard Months. Thus, when the alarm came, it was a shock.

Ariane had been nagging at me for failing to give her the human inputs she needed to complete the Fleet reports on 2378 and 2379, but I had stubbornly refused to be distracted from Mullerium and the bloody tales of the Interregnal period.

My intention was to shorten our sweep of 2380 and use the time thus saved to catch up on our clerical work. Since the white dwarf we were approaching couldn't have any terraforms, I did not think of this as exactly cheating. It is the sort of thing I used to do often as a child, to the dismay of Lady Nora, and it had approximately the same effect on Ariane, who is very conscientious about Fleet busywork.

Ariane had completed the outer zone search on her own, scanning the edges of the PPA and chastising me at the same time. As expected, the region of space subject to Delphinus 2380 inside 500,000,000 kilometers was empty, a true void. Even planetoids and cometary debris had been scoured from the area. It seemed likely that the dense white dwarf star had imploded early in life, sterilizing most of its dependent space.

Somewhere between Nav Julianus's excellent account of the heresy trial of Anselm Styr and his translation of St. Emeric's *Defense of Apostasy,* Ariane said, "We are picking up a line profile of radio emission by neutral hydrogen at twenty-one centimeters in galactic longitude thirty degrees. Shall I file the maxima for retransmission to SW when we are within commo-beacon range?"

I turned slightly on the contour couch and grunted something appropriate. My mind was then a thousand years in time and a million parsecs from Delphinus. I was in the Age of Heroes. I was Nav Anselm on the scaffold; St. Emeric thundering in the cathedral on Algol Epsilon.

Then the alarm sounded, and I came back to reality, surprised to feel my heart suddenly begin to pound under my tunic because I had not heard a danger signal in all this long, long voyage. Ariane was alerted instantly.

"What do you see, Ari?" I demanded.

The computer lights flashed. "Ranging now," Ariane said. "Wait one."

Presently she reported a contact. In this case it was a body of planetoidal size at maximum scan range. Within seconds, Ariane had computed the orbit, "Position now 197,665,000 kilometers from D2380. Apastron is 280,998,000 kilometers, periastron 179,543,000 kilometers. Sidereal period is 83.92 Earth Standard Years. I'll refine that shortly, when we get closer."

The information startled me. Not only was there something in an area of sterilized space, but it was something "planetoidal" in a long period ellipse that brought it perilously close to a white dwarf's radiation belts every eighty-two years. I lowered the lighting on the bridge to red-battle and armored my pod. I brought up the Very Long Range radar display in the console. I could see the familiar stellar scatter associated with radiating dwarfs, but deep in the S-band, I could detect the unmistakable blip of a metallic mass return.

"Ariane," I said. "Recommendations?"

"Deep penetration of the stellar temperate zone with translight cores engaged. I really can't scan effectively at this range." This last remark had a tinge of exasperation in it, as though I were expecting the impossible. At the end of a long survey, Ariane had a tendency to petulance.

"Accepted," I said. "Let's go in. Change to memory mode and record everything. Discharge a message drone at one mega-K intervals." If anything happened to us, the message drones would be picked up eventually by another SW ship or a beacon. "Give me more magnification on the S-band."

The radar image increased in size, but so did the stellar scatter. The nebular mist danced and sparkled. It was beautiful but frustrating.

"How about a holograph?" I asked.

"Not yet," Ariane said.

I would have to wait until the range closed.

"Search the literature," I said.

Ariane was good at this. She responded almost immediately. "In the Draco Nova of 9670, several dark companions to Lambda Draconis were formed, but nothing this small. There's the Nav Chaturgy paper on stellar spume that was given in Algol in '86, but nothing I can scan so far fits the data. Chaturgy was only hypothesizing, in any case. And Nav Setsumi observed librations in Sigma Serpentis back in '16 that suggested a dark companion at a distance of one hundred mega-K. Exploration failed to back his observations. Astrophysicists say that what we are recording now is impossible. The implosion that forms a white dwarf scours the stellar temperate zone. That's the accepted view these days. So much for the literature."

"It wouldn't be the first time the literature was disproved empirically," I said, sounding like an academician.

Ariane let it go. It was her job to believe what was in her memory banks, not to argue about it with the human component of the team.

The air in my pod was growing gelatinous under heavy acceleration. Ariane was closing the contact rapidly. She reported: "The mass return now reads out at approximately one billion metric tons. Too light to be any amount of stellar material. Range closing."

"Too light for a planetoid, too," I said. "Check the unconfirmed SW reports. Maybe there is something there."

Ariane hummed to herself. "A somewhat similar sighting was reported two years ago by Senior Lieutenant Marya Bel-Lorquas and Marcus Cyb-ADSPS-409 in Cygnus. Close recon and flybys were made by Captain Lord Alban in *Bellatrix* and Senior Commander Florian in *Nonesuch*. They reported a tightly grouped cluster of trojan asteroids in balance between Cygnus Beta and Cygnus Beta VI, an ammonia-methane giant. The total mass of the trojans was ten times what we are showing now, and there was a substantial planetary population in the system. That's the only remotely similar case."

"Nothing else in the Fleet banks?"

"No matching natural phenomenon," Ariane said positively.

"Are you suggesting we've picked up something man-made?"

"Insufficient data," Ariane said primly.

Suddenly I had a dreamer's vision of being the discoverer of something truly wonderful in the heart of the galaxy:

perhaps some artifact of the mythical Third Stellar Race.

"Close to one half mega-K," I said, with rising excitement.

Ariane said, "More readings coming in from our probes now. Object is metallic—"

My heart began to thump.

"—metallurgical analysis not possible at this distance. Length is 17,000 meters exactly. Diameter at widest point is 5,000 meters. There goes your dream about discovering the Third Race."

She was absolutely right, as usual. Only a fool would hold out for a system of measurement that would match exactly the metric system human beings had used since long before the first man orbited the home planet.

Then the import of the thing's dimensions penetrated my history-saturated brain. "Are you suggesting we've found an artifact? An artifact seventeen kilometers long and five wide?"

"That seems to be what I am saying," the cyborg declared, sounding exactly like Lady Nora. "Dead mass is 1,000,906,098,006.00752 metric tons. Wait now—I can suppress a bit more of that stellar scurf on the S-band."

The radio image on the display sharpened, and the scatter decreased in intensity. I was looking at a tapered cylinder, familiar in outline, conical on one end, tapered through the waist, and bobtailed. "A starship?" I said unbelievingly. "A starship seventeen kilometers long—?"

"Obviously," Ariane said. "If you think we can risk moving in really close to it, perhaps I can produce something more useful than just information on its size."

"Close the range," I said.

Ariane went to .3 light on a helical approach—what SW pilots called the "skittish corkscrew," a pattern of flight that makes tracking difficult without prior knowledge of the maneuver's foci. It is standard procedure for investigating unknown phenomena in space.

At six million kilometers I shifted the display to Q-band radar holography. A cube representing several hundred thousand cubic kilometers of space materialized in the forward end of my pod. In the star-shot dark floated—the ship.

It was very like the ancient starships in design, but with subtle differences. The angles and curved surfaces were wrong, slightly askew. The starships of the First Empire, the vessels of the Grand Fleet, were beautiful things. Not so this giant cousin. There was something ugly and menacing about it. It brought the short hairs on the back of my neck to attention.

The metal of which it was constructed gave it an extremely low albedo, so that it appeared to blend with the galactic night, a darkness visible mainly because of the background of nebular mist and plasma. The scale of my holograph was too small to pick out details, but there seemed to be odd nodes and spikes dotting the entire surface of the vessel.

I shivered. If such a ship had ever been built in any nation of the Empire, I would have known of it. As an officer of the Imperial Fleet, I could identify almost any vessel in commission in the *known galaxy*. That was the thought that chilled me. I was only too aware of man's tendency to equate the *Empire* with the *galaxy*. Yet no educated man could make such a mistake. The Second Stellar Empire with its nearly nine hundred billion souls occupied only a fractional part of one spiral arm of the immense star cloud known as the Milky Way. And far, far beyond the Rim—that region of the galaxy's edge where the night sky was empty except for the distant luminosity of other, infinitely isolated galaxies—lay the unthinkable stretches of the unknown.

I forced myself to think calmly and logically. That vast ship in the holograph could not have been built by any race of weird aliens. It was a *human* starcraft: different, and built to a titanic scale, but *human*.

I tried to use my historian's sense. I knew that no such giant ship had ever been built by the First Empire. Still there it was: a thousand times bigger than anything ever seen in the galaxy. Enigmatic—and somehow dangerous.

My primitive human instinct, that insight that had brought
the race of men out of Earth's primeval forests and across
the sky, warned me that the black starship was evil.

"Ariane," I said. "What do you think?"

"It's big," she replied with unconscious cyborg banality.

"I can see that," I said irritably. "What else?"

"Period of rotation is 42.995 ESH," she retorted. "And
it penetrates the radiation belts around D2380 at periastron.
If there is protoplasmic life aboard, that could be dangerous
to it. Also, if the thing has a positronic brain it could be
damaged."

"Is there anything alive on board?"

"I can't tell yet," Ariane said. "I'm getting something,
but it could be a harmonic from the solar-phoenix reaction
of D2380."

"You think it is a derelict, then," I suggested.

"That's an ambiguous term," Ariane said primly. "I
wouldn't care to use it."

I sighed and activated the visual scan. Through the now
transparent walls of my pod, I studied the blazing sky of
the galactic center. We were still too far from the object for
any visual sighting. Even D2380 was only a diamond-bright
marble: a small star, even for a white dwarf. But the sky
flamed with stars. It was no wonder, I thought, that the
Order of Navigators had believed starships holy. Men who
flew in space came to mysticism easily, and when the space
pilots of the First Empire founded a religious order to pre-
serve and maintain the ancient starships from the mob furies
of the Interregnum, each generation of priest-Navigators in
turn was given this glorious vision of the stars. Little wonder
they guarded their privileges so fiercely, even (in Talvas's
time) with the rack and the stake. The old religion of star
and starship worship had all but died out in the Empire, but
the Order of Navigators still existed, and there were times
(such as now) when properly brought-up citizens unconsciously wished for their comfort and guidance.

"Range is now forty mega-K," Ariane announced. "I am
going to .1 light. Scanners operating on high gain. Data is

coming in more clearly now." There was an overtone of worry in the cyborg's thoughts. I could sense her deep concern.

"Range is now thirty mega-K. Closing," Ariane said.

"Hold at .1 light and read out the ranges in kilo-K's." As we drew nearer the unknown craft, Ariane and I became more nearly one organism. The interfacing performed at the beginning of our association by the Fleet bio-mechs tended to adjust automatically under stress. In times of great danger the cyborg and I seemed almost telepathically linked.

Ariane was reading out the data from the scans as the range decreased. The information brought a prickling sensation to my flesh. "At range twenty kilo-K we are getting a low level of radiation. Artifact is definitely a starship with protonic controls and old style super-light cores. Cores are apparently intact, but the controls are damaged. Transit systems and protonics are very similar to First Empire designs."

That gave me something to ponder. A starship of a billion metric tons (I could still scarcely credit that figure), a vessel that would tax the resources of a dozen star systems to construct—yet powered by engines of archaic design.

"The control system's main center is shielded. I can't get a really accurate reading. But it is still functioning."

"Could that thing be a robot?" I asked.

"It is likely. Not a true cyborg, in any case. No organic higher systems. But it *has* a brain, of sorts."

"Weapons?"

"Unknown."

"Anything else stirring besides the protonics?"

"Main engines are inert, but undamaged as far as I can tell."

"The center shut them down?"

"It would seem so. Wherever this thing came from, it has definitely arrived in the selected place. The brain damage didn't impair the arrival procedures."

I stirred uneasily in my pod. "Range now?"

"One thousand kilometers coming up on my mark." A pause. "Mark."

"Hold here."

Ariane matched speed and direction to the derelict instantly, inertia dissipated by molecular reversal. It was one of her best maneuvers, and we used it often.

The stars blazed in glory through the transparent shielding of the pod. The sky of the galactic center was like a field of diamonds piled in profusion against the velvet night. I darkened the walls and increased the magnification of the Q-band holograph. At a thousand K it was still impossible to give meaningful scale to the thing in the lasered space. But it was obviously, overpoweringly immense. It blotted out the nebular glow in fully two-thirds of the display. The cold light of the Delphinus star shone on the black hull. I could see that the projections I had noted before girdled the entire vessel. I could not guess at the purpose of the protuberances, but some intuition of mine or Ariane's told me they were part of the great ship's weaponry. The black starcraft was *hostile*—the cyborg and I could both feel it.

Yet the historian in me was stirring. What a find! Warlocks from all over the Empire would want to inspect and study it. The clergy would want a look at it, as well, for though the Order of Navigators was now in the twilight of its great power, it had been the priest-Navigators of the Order who had kept alive the art of starflight and much else during our civilization's Dark Time.

"How far to the next commo beacon?" I asked.

"That is CB-20 in 61 Omicron Draco. Eighteen hours at four kilolights." No starship yet built, not even the ADSPS cyborgs, carried hyperlight radio. The equipment was too bulky. The drones we were launching periodically would home on the nearest commo beacon and dock to transmit their messages—but there was no way we could call for a Fleet vessel directly.

I drew a deep breath and said, "Close the range to five hundred K."

She could tell what was in my mind because we were interfaced. "This really calls for a full-scale expedition,

Kier," the cyborg said. "We should chart it and head for CB-20."

She was absolutely right, of course. She always was. But I was overcome by a huge reluctance to turn our find over to the Grand Fleet without closer inspection. It occurred to me that I was looking at what was probably the most important discovery made in space for the last millennium. I couldn't just chart it and turn away. I *am* a Rhad, after all.

"We will," I said. "After I make a personal survey."

"It could be dangerous," Ariane warned, sounding like Lady Nora again.

"It's a derelict. We have a search and rescue responsibility," I said.

"You know better than that, Starkahn."

"Go to five hundred kilometers," I ordered.

"Order acknowledged," she said, sounding annoyed. "My objections are on the tapes and in the next drone." As usual, she was getting in the last word.

Chapter Two

Beware, O, beware, all you safe and lawful people,
The deathmen, the spellwitches, the weepers
And all the dreadful daemons of the night
Dream of revenge—
Whilst they watch you from The Cloud, *yes!*

> Chant from the *Book of Warls,*
> early Second Stellar Empire period

The crimes committed in the name of a better world
are legion! What if the victims of the Russian Purge
Trials could speak? What if the millions murdered by
Hitler could give tongue to their agony? What if the
descendants of those tortured souls we have con-
demned to the intergalactic night could return to face
us—their tormentors? Should we not tremble?

> Lord Megum, Chairman of the Concerned

Coalition, late First Stellar Empire period.
Tape fragment of a speech found in the ruins
of Tel-Buda, Earth

To approach the great dark ship was like a step backward
into time. I had to remind myself that this was not the age
of Glamiss and Kier the Rebel and Queen Ariane. This was
now—the modern age. Fact, not fear and superstition, ruled.
Not Glamiss the Conqueror, but placid Sokolovsky of
Bellatrix governed the Empire from the Galacton's throne
in Nyor. Not Kier the Rebel, but a council of reasonable
guildsmen directed the destinies of the Rhadan planets. The
cybs and demons with which the Navigators and old warlocks used to frighten grown men and women were half a
millennium out of date. There were no ghosts, and I was a
modern man, an officer of the Fleet, a Rhadan nobleman
and an educated person. Still, the dreadful ship made my
blood run cold.

At the reduced distance I had to lower the magnification
of the Q-band holograph to keep the dark spaceship within
the confines of my pod. It hung against the luminous sky,
rotating ponderously, as enigmatic as the ruins of Astraris
or the Sphinx.

There were no ports or transparent surfaces that I could
see. But there was nothing remarkable about that. Few of
the ancient starships had glassine decks.

"Any better readings?" I asked.

"Mass distribution is interesting," Ariane said. "That thing
is almost solid."

"Solid? How could that be?"

"The entire hull is packed with protonic and nucleonic
hardware. The logic cards alone must number in the quin-
tillions," Ariane said. "I don't know, Kier. The whole thing
gives me a bad feeling. The ship is practically one immense
space-born computer. I don't know why I think so—call it
female intuition if you like—but I think it is some sort of
war-games device. A weapons system."

I tried to digest that, still staring at the holograph of the

monstrous black hulk. "There are no life-support systems?
No crew areas?"

"None. The entire vessel seems to be automatic, guided
by a low order of intelligence in the protonics. Wait, one.
I'm getting a low-level sensor reading on the scan. Hold
while I compute."

I drew an uneasy breath, and presently Ariane spoke
again. "There is one free passageway leading to what seems
to be a special area in the central core. But the chamber is
only two meters by two meters by four meters. Except for
that and the access passage, the hull is packed solid with
circuitry and machines."

"Close to fifty kilometers," I said, my throat dry.

"Acknowledged," the cyborg replied. No protest this time.

I shut down the holography, and the walls of my pod
grew transparent once again. I watched as the growing bulk
of the dark starship blotted out the Delphinus star. I could
feel Ariane maneuvering, tacking against the drift of the
plasma winds from the white dwarf.

At fifty kilometers the strange vessel's size became over-
powering. It was one thing to see the derelict's holographic
image inside my pod, it was quite another to see the thing
itself, as long as the island of Tel-Manhat, blotting out the
sky. We seemed, even at this distance, to be under the curve
of the great hull.

"Kier," Ariane said suddenly. "I am picking up some
indications of power consumption. Very low. Less than a
thousandth of an ampere. But it is there. The readout in-
dicates some sort of life-support system. Not more than one
meter by two meters. Very sophisticated. And it seems to-
tally independent of the main power sources aboard and
distinct from the positronics."

I had the squeamish feeling that Ariane was describing
some sort of coffin, and I was about to comment when the
ship's rotation slowly brought into view an open portal.

The nebular glow painted the nightside of the hull with
a vague, silvery light. But the portal was distinct: a darker
darkness against the black bulk of the ship. I raised the

magnification of the walls and zoomed in on the opening. It was exactly that, an opening. No hatch, no airlock—just an open hole.

"Probe that, Ariane," I said anxiously.

"It's just what it appears to be, Kier. An ingress-egress port. Completely open to space."

Now I knew (if I had ever doubted it) that I should chart the derelict's position and make for CB-20 at Ariane's best speed. But that open portal drew me. I was, after all, twenty and the Starkahn of Rhada, and I lived in an age that offered little in the way of opportunities for grand gestures and gallantry. Bookish I was, but I was the descendant of warrior star kings and the son of a Great Vegan noblewoman. Personal bravery was expected of me.

What I planned now was not bravery, of course. It was sheer folly—and Ariane said so.

"You can't be serious," she said, sounding very feminine. "You simply can*not* be serious."

"I am," I said, trying to sound masterful and commanding.

"I won't permit it," she declared.

I drew a deep breath, nerved myself, and said, "I am in command." It was quite true. Ariane's fleet rank was ensign, a single sunburst to my two as a sublieutenant. This was not always the case. In several of the Survey teams, the cyborg held the higher rank. Ariane had to defer to me. But as a free citizen of the Empire, she had the right to enter her protests on the log tapes. This was a privilege she exercised often, and she did it now.

"I am making a copy for the Lady Nora, as well," she said threateningly.

"We'll see about that," I said hotly. "Those tapes are classified as of now."

"Protest," Ariane said sharply.

"Noted," I said, tight-lipped. Probably if Ariane hadn't threatened to "tell my mother on me," I might have reconsidered. There was actually very little I could accomplish by boarding the derelict, and sober second thoughts about penetrating that grim and enigmatic monster were chilling my desire for glory. But there was no turning back now. "It is decided," I said.

I could feel the computer working again. She was probably searching Fleet regulations for some way to prevent me going EV in a tactically questionable situation. But there would be nothing. The Grand Fleet still operated on the regulations and Noble Code written when the military took over the starships from the Order of Navigators. My single sunburst advantage in rank made me warleader, lord, king and master of our little two-person ecology.

"There's nothing in the Regs, is there?" I asked.

"No," Ariane said.

"So?"

"Very well, Starkahn," she said. She was sulking, no doubt of it.

"Take us in to one kilometer while I suit up," I said, feeling masterful and vindicated: a true descendant of Kier the Rebel.

Chapter Three

The legends say that there were those among the great of the Golden Age who determined to cleanse the race of all foulness, and to this purpose sent into darkness millions: some guilty, some innocent, all embittered.

The legends say this, and so do the Warls. But of my own knowledge, I cannot tell whether or not this monstrous tale is true.

Nav (Bishop) Julianus Mullerium,
Anticlericalism in the Age of the Star Kings,
middle Second Stellar Empire period

Before the founding of our Order, there was undoubtedly great glory. What was lacking was conscience.

Attributed to St. Emeric of Rhada,
Grand Master of Navigators,
early Second Stellar Empire period

And so it was that I found myself slowly free-falling through the dark shaft into the heart of the derelict starship. When I left the "surface," I did so with dread. But with the exercise of the mental discipline I had learned in my seven grimly confining years at the Fleet Academy, I managed to bring myself out of my funk.

The fact was that there seemed, at the moment at least, little enough to be frightened about. In the absorbing darkness there was very little sensation of falling, or of movement of any sort. Then there was Ariane's comforting presence, for we soon discovered that the E-phone functioned perfectly through the metal and shielding of the derelict.

I was suffering from a mild claustrophobia in the passageway. I moved "downward" in an egg of light from my suit lamps. High "above" me I could still see the tiny opening dusted with stars. Then I reached an angle in the shaft, and the patch of sky vanished.

Ariane spoke to me. "Something has taken note of you. I am getting some protonic leakage. Very low level, but it wasn't there before. Suggest you return."

I swallowed to ease the rusty taste in my throat and said, "Noted. Just a bit farther. Keep me informed."

Later, it seemed hours but it was only seconds, Ariane said, "No change."

At least whatever it was took no overt action against my penetration of the ship. Perhaps, I thought, it wasn't intended to.

I didn't like it. I decided to go for one minute more and then abandon my exploration. I told Ariane so.

"Keep sending," she said. "Talk."

"I am moving now. This place is black as hell. I must be a good two kilometers inside and still nothing but this shaft. I'll go on for thirty seconds more and then I'll—" I stopped abruptly. Ariane immediately demanded to know what was happening.

But nothing was happening at all. I had come up against a blank wall. I oriented myself, standing on a side wall, and stared, stunned by the anticlimax of it. An open passageway leading into the gut of the huge vessel, and now this—a wall.

I described it to Ariane.

"Not logical," she said shortly.

"Nevertheless," I said, annoyed.

"There must be a way through. The life-support system I scanned is just past it."

I turned up my suit lamps and saw the symbols. They formed a single word. The letters were spiny and archaic: almost, but not quite, the characters of First Empire Anglic. The word was a simple instruction. *Touch.*

Who etched that word into the black metal? And how long ago? And by all the cybs and little demons, where?

I touched the wall with my gloved hand. A valve dilated swiftly. A simple pressure latch. There were valves that operated that way on the antique starships of the Grand Fleet.

Ahead of me lay the room Ariane had described after the scan. It was as featureless as the shaft had been—except for one thing. In the light of the suit lamps, I could see a crystal pod, a cylinder. Metal containers were affixed to both ends and the whole latched to the deck with two metal straps. My suit radiation counter was registering the low count associated with nuclear clocks. I energized the scan camera so that Ariane could see what I was seeing. Ariane said immediately, "The radiation is snowing the picture. I can't see clearly." I described my surroundings. "The whole room is so *simple*. There's nothing on the walls. No controls of any sort."

"The ship is automatic. That room has nothing to do with the rest of it. It's a passenger cove," Ariane said. "Investigate that pod."

I could see that the cylinder was independent of the ship but for a single power lead. Except for that and the metal straps, the capsule could float free in the near null-gravity. I settled to the proper floor and moved into the center of the room. My lamps cast their light down on the crystal

pod. My heartbeat went wild, and Ariane, guarding the
biosensors, immediately demanded to know what was wrong.
"What do you see?"

But I had no words to describe what I was seeing.

The cylinder was filled with some sort of clear liquid,
gently in motion. And within, floating in amniotic repose,
lay the "alien."

I unconsciously made the sign of the Star. I am not really
very religious, but it seemed the proper thing to do, under
the circumstances.

The alien was a woman. A girl, really, though I had no
way to guess at her age. Her age! What was I thinking?
She must have lain, naked and gently moving, in that life-
supporting pod for—how long? Holy Star and St. Emeric,
how long? A thousand years? Two? Longer. Probably much
longer. How long is eternity?

Dark hair floated about her pale oval face. She was beautiful—and frightening. I felt an icy chill as I realized she
was looking at me. Her eyes were open, and they were the
strangest eyes I have ever seen. They were the color of
newly minted silver. There was no iris, only the silver sheen
of the eyeball, pierced by a tightly contracted slit pupil. She
was *not* human. Not completely so, in any case. A mutant.
And, of course, she was not looking at me at all. She lay
in a death sleep in that chrysalis: beautiful, uncannily
strange—but alive. As I stared in rapt fascination, I could
see a pulse beat in her throat. Once every minute and a half
it gently throbbed.

After a long while I reported to Ariane, never taking my
eyes from the silver-eyed girl.

"Kier!"

It took me a moment to awaken from my dream.

"Kier!"

Cyborgs are said to have rather phlegmatic tempera-
ments, but there was nothing calm or placid about the emotions Ariane was feeling at this moment. Her concern was
so strong that it was feeding back to me through my own
biosensors and the encephalophone contacts. In a human

being it would have been fear, even terror, but cyborg emotive functions are not human. They respond differently (and, I think, more efficiently) to danger.

"Something is happening to that ship, Kier! I want you out of there—*now!*"

"What is it?"

"The drive cores are heating up. And there is some sort of radiation screen building. I don't know how much longer I'll be able to maintain contact. Get out of there fast."

Something—perhaps my presence—was activating the black starship. I stood for a moment, torn by indecision. If the cores were warming, the vessel could go into translight mode at any moment. In minutes, the ship and all it contained could be moving at an unknown number of kilolights across space in intersystem transit—if it didn't disintegrate into fissioning atoms, torn apart by the gravitational field of the Delphinus star.

But could I simply decamp, leaving the life-support capsule—the most important find of centuries? At that moment I only knew that I wasn't going to leave the derelict by myself.

"Ariane!" I called. "Can I feed this capsule from my suit batteries?"

The cyborg didn't waste time arguing with me. She came back with an instantaneous computation. "Plug the power lead into your biosensor bank. The contacts won't match, but there should be enough leakage to keep it going for a few minutes while you get back here. Only make it fast, Kier. There's an ionization corona forming around the core projections. You haven't much time."

I unlatched the metal straps holding the capsule to the deck and pulled the power lead free. Next I disconnected my biosensors and jammed the lead into my suit batteries. I glanced at the valve and saw with a flash of incipient panic that it was contracting.

For a nonathlete, soft from months of low-gravity living, I moved with remarkable speed. I wrapped myself around the crystal cylinder and burned my suit thrusters all in one movement. We crashed through the closing valve and caromed silently off the wall of the open shaft. The jar set my head to ringing, but I managed to orient myself properly and plunged up the corridor at full thrust, riding the life-support capsule like a war mare. Twice during that plunging flight the capsule struck the sides of the shaft and almost started tumbling. At our speed it would have been fatal, but I straightened out, lighting the walls with the thruster flames, until I could see the sky overhead. The ionization corona, the mark of a starship making ready to move, had spread from the core projections kilometers away at the stern. It shimmered over the skin of the vessel like swampfire.

"Kier—" Ariane's transmission was faint, blocked by an increasing hiss of core harmonics. "There's a rising level of activity in the positronic banks. I can't translate, but I'm taping everything I can. Hurry!"

In moments the great starship would vanish into inter-system transit. When it was gone from this place, assuming it didn't go off like a planet-sized bomb, what hope would there be of our ever finding it again? "Ariane!" I called. "Stop it. Put a fish into the stern cores!" The damage a nuclear torpedo would do striking the stern of the monster ship would be considerable—but better that than to lose such a find forever.

"When you are clear." Ariane's transmission was barely readable.

At that instant I burst from the open portal into space, straddling the alien cylinder. The ship had rotated and I was in the direct glare of D2380, and for a second or two I was disoriented. Then I caught sight of Ariane, silvery against the dust of stars, and I thrust in her direction with all the power in my suit.

I was tumbling, and I could see the great sheets of light, like an aurora, playing off the metal surfaces of the monster. *"Shoot!"* I ordered, and Ariane responded immediately. I caught only the briefest glimpse of the nuclear torpedo, a meter in diameter and three meters long, streaking for the target like a miniature starship.

The great starship vanished. As it went hyper-light, the vast volume of space it had occupied imploded with soundless violence. Streamers of glowing plasma formed, swirling into nebular shapes. Ariane and I and the alien capsule tumbled inward toward the heart of the torn space and then were flung outward, like leaves in a whirlpool. The stars streaked in my field of vision. I could feel my body fluids surging this way and that under the sudden and unpredictable G-loads. I lost my hold on the capsule, and it went spinning off. Ariane's nuclear torpedo reached the spot where its intended target had been and exploded in white flare, adding to the confusion and disruption.

I must have lost consciousness for a few moments because when I opened my aching eyes again, Ariane was very nearby, her hatch open and her crane extended to hook me in. The capsule was already aboard, the snapped power lead tangled in coils on the airlock deck. A reflection inside my helmet made me turn as the polarized shield snapped over my eyes. The glittering arc light of the Delphinus star was brightening. It was impossible, but it was happening. A million-mile stellar flare formed, and once again the plasmas swirled around us. I could see the shape of the star distorting. Something had shattered the photosphere, and the flaming guts of the star were boiling into space.

"Ariane!" I yelled. "What's happening to it?"

I felt the cyborg lay hold of me with her crane, gentle as a mother. She drew me into the lock. *"The star,"* I said confusedly, *"what's happening to the star?"*

The hatch closed, and I could feel the jolt of high acceleration—much higher acceleration that I ever remembered Ariane using while a human was aboard her. I felt as though I were being squashed inside my suit, like an insect in its shell. Then came the familiar disorientation of a fast shift into hyper-light speed. The surge was powerful, and it lasted a full six seconds. Ariane was traveling away from D2380 at two kilolights or more. Panic speed.

Then I realized what had happened, even though the cyborg was too busy saving our lives to take the time to tell me.

The black starship had done something—something impossible according to any science *we* knew. The alien starship had done something, and the star was going nova.

Chapter Four

*(Who knows) what song the Sirens sang, or what name
Achilles assumed when he hid himself among the
women?*

Dawn Age fragment found at Tel-London,
attributed to Sir Thomas Browne
(1603-1665 Old Style)

*The actions of the young sometimes seem ill-considered
and foolish, but should we not await the judgment of
history?*

St. Emeric of Rhada, *The Dialogues*,
early Second Stellar Empire period

I had to face the ordeal of a military Court of Inquiry for
the "loss" of the black starship, for endangering "by poor

astronautical judgment" the life of one Ariane Cyb-ADSPS 339, "a citizen of the Empire," and—just incidentally— my own.

There were two captains, three commodores, and an admiral on the board, and they were a grim lot, for all their silver braid and medal ribbons. Alt-Romul, the Altairi Commodore, held out for a full court martial to be conducted at Nyor—which would have made a circus of the whole business. I had my noble ancestry to thank for that suggestion. Alt-Romul is descended from the Interregnal kings of Novorome, a planet subdued (with no great gentleness) by Kier the Rebel in Glamiss Magnificio's time. So long do our Empire nobles cling to ancient blood feuds.

Fortunately for me (and, I hope, for the cause of military justice), Admiral the Honorable Morag O'Kane Macdonald had gone to school with the Lady Nora at Tel-Lausanne about thirty years ago, and she spoke for me and put the Altairi inquisitor in his place. It is custom, though not law, in the Empire that any man must face judgment by his peers. And this has come to mean, over the centuries, that a Rhad must be tried in Rhada, just as a Veg would be tried in Great Vega or an Altairi in the Alt Confederacy.

The court held several sessions at the New Kynan Fleet base, where Ariane was resting, so that she could testify, and I think it was her account of our encounter in Delphinus that saved me. That, and Lady Nora, and the stern-faced old maiden admiral who reminded the noble court of ancient privileges and prerogatives. All women, of course. The men on the board wanted to hang me.

In the end I received a reprimand for my conduct. It declared that I had used poor judgment in venturing into the black starship, that I had deviated from standing orders for such contacts, and that I had violated Fleet regulations in removing "an artifact" from the derelict. They couldn't bring themselves to refer to the girl in the life-support capsule as *an alien*. I was further reprimanded for bringing "the artifact" to Rhada rather than to my Fleet base. But I refused to be dismayed by that part of the reprimand. The alien girl was resting now in the hands of the warlocks of the University of Gonlanburg rather than in some triple-security military prison-cum-experimental laboratory, and custom being what it was in the Empire, it seemed unlikely that the government at Nyor would demand Rhada surrender her to them, though an unnecessary number of security troops had now descended on the quiet campus of the Gonlani-Rhad school.

My trial lasted three weeks, and during that time no attempt had been made by the warlocks to awaken the death-sleeping alien in the capsule. The fluid in which she floated had been analyzed, the systems of the capsule had been studied, and very great number of highly educated men had made guesses about her age and origin—but that was all.

For myself—well, one would have thought I had enough to worry about, even after the adjournment of the court, so that I wouldn't keep thinking about the girl in the capsule—but it didn't work out like that. I spent hours each day thinking about her: trying to imagine whence she had come, trying to grasp in some way the secrets that must lie within that sleeping mind. At least, I *thought* it was sleeping. Some of the learned warlocks at Gonlanburg contended that a long coma, no matter how induced or supported, would inevitably destroy brain tissue. That would leave my beautiful alien some sort of preserved vegetable, her secrets locked up forever. I couldn't believe that.

In Rhada we tend to be a bit more religious than in the nations of the galactic center, probably because we are a Rim planet. When one can see the shapes of the galactic lens so clearly in the darkness of the night, one tends to glorify the unknown powers of God and the holy Star spirit. So it was inevitable that the clergy, the Order of Navigators, should be consulted on the theological aspects of the alien in the laboratories in Gonlanburg. Priest-Navs of all the medical disciplines gathered at the university to study and to give tongue to their opinions. I learned of all this second hand, through friends at the university, for after the court adjourned, I was put on leave from the Survey Wing (this was the brass's way of preserving me while they decided what to do with a reprimanded Fleet officer who was also hereditary warleader and Starkahn of Rhada).

Ariane was refitted at New Kynan and given leave, too. She chose to spend her rest period playing manta in the Gonlan Sea. I think she did it for me, knowing I'd want someone on Gonlan while I paid my respectful duty to Lady Nora on the home estates in Rhada. Ariane called me by hyperphone every three days to keep me informed about what was happening to the silver-eyed girl in the capsule. "After all," Ariane explained, "she is as much *my* responsibility as she is *yours,* Starkahn." I didn't know what to make of such remarks, but I was glad she took the trouble to report to me.

On the twelfth day of Iceblue, our coldest month on Rhada, Ariane called me to say that the weather was warm and balmy on the Gonlanburg coast, that the sea was clear and the diving good, and that, incidentally, a commission of warlocks and Navigators had recommended that the university medical staff attempt to revive the alien girl within a month or less, since the power sources available did not match exactly the systems of the life-support capsule and they feared a malfunction might produce irreversible damage. "They say they have to take a chance on revival," Ariane reported, "because the starship is gone and, well, you know the rest of it—"

I did, indeed, know the rest of it. If they tried and failed to revive the alien girl, I would be forever damned as the idiot who had killed mankind's only contact with whatever mysterious branch of the race had created the vast technology that had produced the greatest starship ever heard of in the main galaxy.

"Reserve accommodations for me at Zodiac Bay," I told Ariane. "I have to be there when the magicians try to wake her."

"Not a sensible decision, Starkahn," Ariane said. "But more like you than skulking about at home nursing your wounds. I will expect you in thirty hours."

As I rang off, I became conscious of the Lady Nora watching me. She stood in the doorway of my suite, looking statuesque and quite properly framed by the ancient stones of the archway.

"That was Ariane, I suppose," she said.

"Yes, Lady Mother," I replied formally and politely, like a well-brought-up child. The truth was that I always felt a bit like a child in Lady Nora's presence. She was certainly one of the most beautiful women of the Empire, even though she was close to seventy years old. She had never undergone geri-genesis, and consequently she hadn't that parchment-skin quality that old reborns get. In an earlier age, Lady Nora would have passed easily for a woman in her early thirties—perhaps even younger than that. One must remember that she is a noblewoman of the Empire: a personage who has never known a day's want or an hour's hardship. Yet, for all of that, Lady Nora is typical of the great ladies of our time—all of them descendants of generations of warrior queens who helped their men tame not nations, but whole star systems. Pampered she might be, but she was made of stern stuff.

She swept into the room (not meaning to, but unable to move without the grace and power of a starship of the line) and began her interrogation. "Ariane is well?" Fruitless question. She knew perfectly how well Ariane was at the moment, as well as where she was and how she was spending her leave.

"Yes, Lady Mother," I said. "I was thinking of joining her at Gonlanburg."

Nora frowned. "You want to go off-world so soon? You have barely gotten home, Kier."

She meant "home" to the estate, not home to Rhada. She was too tactful to mention the weeks of the military inquiry.

"Tell me about the creature you captured, Kier," she said, settling on a formless chair that rose to greet her.

"I didn't exactly 'capture' her, Mother," I said cautiously.

"I understand she was very lovely. Exotic, of course. One expects that. But physically quite—appealing."

I suppressed an urge to smile at that. Mother is a Great Vegan, and Vegans are notoriously prudish. The fact that the alien girl had lain naked within her life-support capsule would have already been reported to the Lady Nora, who would somehow feel this reflected discredit on whatever strange and alien culture dispatched the girl and the black starship on their incomprehensible mission.

"Quite appealing, Lady Mother," I said.

"Ariane said 'beautiful.' Yes, I think that was the word she used."

Ah, I thought, *the mysterious female ways of my cyborg alter-ego.* Was it possible for a slip of a girl of fifteen metric tons to be jealous in the ordinary female way? *Devious,* she was. Of *that* I could be absolutely certain.

"Well," I said. "I suppose one *might*—in certain circumstances—think the girl was beautiful, Lady Mother."

"Silver eyes, I am told." Lady Nora had been told a good deal, and about things more significant than the color of an alien's eyes.

"Yes. Silver," I said, remembering them with a shiver— the way she seemed to be looking at me through that liquid-filled chrysalis.

"Unusual," Lady Nora murmured. "But scarcely unique. There are silver-eyed blacks on Bellatrix Delta V." My mother settled the embroidered panels of her gown about her so that she looked even more regal, very much a part of the old room in the ancient house of the Rhadan kings. "Kier," she said, regarding me with steady, cobalt-blue eyes, "you know that there are some members of our family who consider me a domineering woman..."

"Surely not, Mother," I said with gentle irony.

"Oh, yes," she went on with classic disregard of my small thrust. "Your granduncle of Aurora, for example. And all of his kin. Marfan of Xanthis, Kreon, all the Melissande connections. In fact, almost all of *that* side of the family—"

"Father's relatives," I said.

"Quite so. Your father's kinfolk. All rather socialist in

their leanings for nobles of the Empire, you know. Your father was a dear man, and I loved him very much, Kier. But he never lived up to his breeding, not as he should have. He was warleader and star king, after all."

"He was Starkahn of the Rhadan Republic, Lady Nora," I said with a coolness of formality in my tone. I knew what was coming, more or less, and I wanted to prevent an argument if possible. The Lady Nora was a royalist to her fingertips. I could not imagine that she would ever become involved in active treason against the Republic, but one could not avoid knowing where her sympathies lay—nor could not escape her aristocratic conviction that every event, every chance, should be exploited toward a restoration of the old regime.

"Starkahn, then," my mother said scornfully. "*We* know what the title means, you and I, Kier. And so do plenty of others. Including the Galacton."

She was right about that, in any case. There was always a strong royalist movement in Rhada. The Republic had only come about because of the dilution of this sympathy by the populations of Aurora and Xanthis and the other principalities forcibly welded to the Palatinate by my warrior ancestors. They had, in effect, brought about the downfall of our family dynasty by their own success in war. But the royalist party remained strong on the home world, and everyone knew that a royalist coup on Rhada would bring no reprisals or interference from the heir of great Glamiss who ruled as Galacton in Nyor. So long as Rhada remained loyal to the Empire, it mattered to no one outside the former Palatinate whether Rhada were monarchy or republic.

But the royalist movement on Rhada, though strong, had always been small, and it had one other great disadvantage. It had *me* as heir presumptive to the feathered cape and golden regalia of star king.

And now? I wondered. Since the Court of Inquiry, I had remained in seclusion. But the Lady Nora's attitude suggested that perhaps something had changed to make the royalist cause stronger. I dreaded the possibility.

"I am sorry you are choosing this particular time to go off-world Kier," she said. "Your people have had very little chance to become reacquainted with you." Mother had a way of making it sound as though all Rhadans were tenants on some huge farm owned by the family.

"'My people' as you call them, Mother, have always thought me a bit of a twit. They can hardly have changed that opinion," I said.

"They have thought you perhaps a bit overly studious, Kier. But they have always loved you."

"The Rhad don't love anyone who isn't cast in the heroic mold, my Lady Mother, and you know it well. I've always been 'that book-bagging Rhad.' Nose pinned to a tape-viewer. All that." I had my moments of *wishing* the Rhad saw me as some sort of reincarnation of Kier the Rebel. But they didn't. There was no use pretending about it.

Lady Nora said, "The story of the manner in which you went alone into the strange starship and captured the alien is common knowledge in the Palatinate by now, Kier. The people are pleased."

I had to smile at that. "Are you suggesting I'm some sort of hero?"

"The Rhad like bravery," Lady Nora declared.

"But what I did wasn't particularly brave. It wasn't even very clever. The starship is gone, and the *alien* was only a girl in a life-support capsule—a girl who was quite out of it, by the way. Hardly able to defend herself, if it comes to that. The Court of Inquiry thought I was more stupid than heroic."

Lady Nora wasn't going to accept that. "You have been out of touch with people these last few days. Your story is well known in Rhada—"

Trust my mother for *that*—

"—it has the makings of a guest song: how you tried to take the black starship singlehanded and how it blasted the Delphinus star."

"Mother," I protested. "We don't *know* that the starship had anything to do with the nova."

"You haven't heard, then."

"Heard what?"

"The great ship was sighted again. In Libra. Sigma Libra went nova within three ESH of the sighting."

I was appalled in the evident satisfaction Lady Nora took from this news. The Sigma Libra system was uninhabited except for a small commo-station on the farthermost planet, but the loss of life could have been enormous if the black starship had struck elsewhere. I felt out of my depth and in need of allies. My mother often made me feel this way, but this was no simple family matter. Plainly, the situation was out of hand. The Empire was in danger—and the aristocrats like Lady Nora refused to see anything more in the events of the last weeks than an opportunity to play politics.

"I shall consult Gret," I said. The Royal Vulk, with his wisdom of millennia, would know what must be done.

"*You* are the Starkahn. Not Gret." Did I detect a note of anti-Vulkish prejudice there? I hoped not.

"And Rhada is a republic, Mother. The age of the star kings is over here on the Rim."

Lady Nora's eyes flashed angrily. "Don't talk to me like a shopkeeper, Kier. Your responsibility—"

I cut her off with unaccustomed abruptness. "You have just told me that an attack of some sort, delivered by means unfamiliar to us, has destroyed a stellar outpost of the Empire. Yet in the same breath you seem to suggest I should stay home and play at plotting to bring back the monarchy. Mother, what are you dreaming of? I am Fleet officer of the Empire—"

"You are the Starkahn of Rhada."

"I am a citizen of the Rhadan Republic, madam. And so are you. Our duty is to protect the state and the Empire of which it is a part—not to try to overturn it."

My mother regarded me coldly, as though I were some stranger who had found his way into her home by mistake and against her wishes. "It has always been my belief that it was a mistake to allow your education to be overseen by the Vulk. Now I am even more certain of it. Your father wished it so because it is a tradition in the family. Very well. Seek counsel where you will. I respect Gret for what he has been to the noble/Rhad since the first star king's time. I do *not* accept his notions of universal brotherhood and equality. Now you may do as you see fit."

With that cold pronouncement, Lady Nora Veg-Rhad, *quondam* princess of Rhada and Great Vega, swept from the room more regally than any present-day Galacton. Regretfully, I watched her go—and my thoughts turned to my tutor, Gret.

To understand Rhadans, one must also understand the Vulk and their relation to us as a people. Only once, in all the millennia of star-voyaging, has man discovered another intelligent race. The first contact between humans and the Vulk is lost in the mists of antiquity. They are a strange people, small of stature, humanoid, but very different from men. Within their bulging skulls lie brains with almost mystical powers of telepathy and mind-sharing. Lacking eyes and ears, they do not see as men do. In ancient times men believed they "saw" men's souls. And during the Dark Time, millions of Vulks paid for men's fears and superstitions with their lives.

It is strange that even after thousands of years of living with the Vulk, men know so little of them. Their home world was destroyed in some celestial catastrophe, yet there are still thousands of them scattered through the reaches of the Empire. They are not male and female as men are, yet they have a counterpart of sex. Gret, my tutor, for example, had lived much of his life with a consort, Erit.

Among the Rhad there is an ancient custom called Triad, established, some say, by my ancestor Kier the Rebel. This is a mind-link among two Vulk and a human being. It is a clumsy thing, according to the Vulk, because man's mind is not yet sufficiently developed for true telepathy. But it is by Triad that much instruction is given to the Rhadan young. It lends itself as a technique for teaching history—for the Vulk are extremely long-lived. Some say twenty thousand years, perhaps even longer.

Gret, the Royal Vulk of Rhada, had grown old in the

service of my family. He knew Kier the Rebel and the glorious Queen Ariane. He knew Kynan the Navigator, Star King of the Gonlani-Rhad, who some say might have been Galacton had he chosen to be, eight hundred years ago. Gret was my father's friend and my teacher, and, some said, the wisest creature in Rhada. It was to him I felt I must now turn.

Chapter Five

—and it is my wish that my descendants honor this Patent while the House of Rhad rules in Rhada. The Vulk known to men as Gret has been my honored friend and my father's friend. My trust in him is complete. . . . For howsoever long the Vulk Gret wishes to serve the House of Rhad, let him be known as Royal Vulk to this family. Given this thirtieth day of the seventh month of the year 6,001 Galactic Era: this sixtieth year of my reign as Kier, second star king of Rhada.

> Excerpt from a Patent of Nobility,
> the Rhadan archives,
> early Second Stellar Empire period

Fear the Vulk, for he sees without eyes and knows the Black Arts and dreams of the blood of children. He is not as men are.

From *The Vulk Protocols*, authorship unknown,
Interregnal period

*How little we really know of the Vulk. We believe that
he lives long, that he touches minds, that he loves
men. We do not know how long, or if he really knows
our thoughts, or why he should love us. Of this alone
we are certain: in ten thousand years of star-voyaging,
only the Vulk have we found sharing our eternity.*
Mattias ben Mullerium,
Vulkish Customs Among the Rhad,
late Second Stellar Empire period

The room wherein I found my old tutor was scarcely to be
considered a "room" at all. It was, in its fashion, a life-
support system, for Gret was incredibly old, even for a Vulk.

The air was warm and moist, the light dim, the air pressure slightly lower than normal for Rhada. The environ-
mental controls were set to simulate, as nearly as possible,
the conditions of Vulka—a world that had ceased to be six
thousand years before the Second Empire was born.

Gret lay in his tank, a wizened and naked humanoid
form: large-headed, without features save for the small and
sensitive mouth. The slender hands and tiny, flexible fingers
floated in the clear gel within the tank. Gret now spent half
of his waking hours in nutrient gels. He could no longer
eat even the minute amounts needed to sustain life in a
Vulk.

Yet this feeble creature had once ridden with Kier the
Rebel into Nyor, challenging the power of the usurping
Empress Marlana and the cyborg star king, Tallan. My sense
of history and the past was excited by the thought of the
memories contained within that bulging Vulkish skull, memories that encompassed three-fifths of man's history as a
star-voyaging race.

Somewhere in the dimness, the changing pressures caused
by my arrival in Gret's chamber struck a whispering har-

monic from the old Vulk's lyre. The titanium and silver
strings, pegged to the carved horn by artisans who lived
under Vulka's triple sun, hummed and shimmered.

I said formally, "I greet you, Magister."

I felt the mind-touch. A warm affection, the gelid caress
of the fluids in Gret's tank, a ghostly image of the blazing,
colored life-auras by which the Vulk "saw." I realized that
I was "seeing" myself, a feeble reflection of the coruscating
figure in my old teacher's mind. It was a familiar experience,
but always an eerie one.

"I have been expecting you," Gret said.

"I would have come sooner, but there were problems."
The Vulk was too old and feeble to be plagued with my
troubles with the Fleet, with Lady Nora, and all the rest of
it.

But, of course, he knew about all of it. A Vulk was never
isolated—not as long as another of his kind was within
range of the remarkable powers of his mind.

"When I learned of it, Kier," Gret said, "I sent Erit to
Gonlan."

I was touched and disturbed, as well. In recent years it
had not been Gret's way to send his sister-wife, the younger
Erit, a-roaming—even to gather information. They, the two
of them, had spent millennia roving space in the service of
the Rhad family, and now they had come to the time of
taking their ease as Royal Vulk and his consort. So Gret
must have been deeply worried to send Erit to Gonlan, where
the warlocks were gathering to decide what must be done
about the alien from the black starship.

"You should not have sent her away from you, Magister,"
I said respectfully. "The troubles will resolve themselves."

"Not these troubles, my young friend." Gret's thoughts,
perfectly clear and disciplined, murmured in my mind.

"Your sister-wife is at the university?" I asked.

"She is with the warlocks," Gret replied. "They could
not deny her." Even today, there is prejudice against the
Vulk, and in some places among the Inner Nations, a Vulk

would not be permitted on the scene of sensitive and secret investigations. But in Rhada, no one would exclude the Vulk Erit, who was consort to the tutor of the nation's royal princes. "The warlocks are going to attempt to revive the alien girl you brought to Rhada. They ask that Erit attempt to probe her mind—if she survives the awakening."

I said directly, then, what had been troubling me for days now. "The starship Ariane and I discovered in Delphinus— it is a doomsday machine, isn't it?"

"I believe it to be one," Gret said.

I cast about the chamber, suddenly tormented by the threat brought into the Empire by my rashness. "But *why*, Gret? And *who*? Who would build such a machine? It would take the resources of a star system and a lifetime. And for what? To build something so destructive is madness. Even in war, such a ship would—" I broke off, unable to find words to express my bafflement.

"—be useless," Gret finished for me. "Yes, I know."

"Then who? Why?"

"I cannot answer that. But perhaps Erit will, when the alien is awakened."

I thought of the silver-eyed girl in the capsule, and then I remembered the way the Delphinus star had vaporized. In the heart of the galaxy, it was still expanding, scouring life from its quadrant of space. And the warmen at the Fleet commo station on the Sigma Libra planet—what had they thought when their sky began to burn?

"Your Lady Mother is certain that the starship attacked Sigma Libra. She relishes the idea," Gret said disapprovingly.

"Is there any doubt?"

"None. It was the starship, without question."

"Then Lady Nora—" I began defensively.

Gret cut me off. "She is a noblewoman, is Lady Nora. She lives in the past." I felt the Vulk's dry tolerance. "As you do, young Starkahn, as you do. But there's a difference. You dream of past glories. She would use present horror to bring back those past glories she so relishes."

The Lady of Rhada might be proud, but she was no monster, and I said so, angrily.

"Forgive me, Starkahn," Gret said. "It is that I have seen so much pain and grief come from ambition. Your mother wants the black starship to remain a mystery, a larger-than-life fear. You—and *only* you have been aboard it. What greater heroism can there be? You know how the Rim loves personal bravery. The Royalists are delighted with you."

"I wouldn't have it so if I had a choice, Magister," I said humbly. "I am no star king."

"Perhaps so, perhaps not," the Vulk said. "But what is far more important than our small politics here in the hinterlands is the fact that a doomsday machine is loose in the galaxy. If the next Delphinus or Sigma Libra should be one of the Inner Nations—billions could die."

"That is why I've come to you," I said. "I must go to Gonlan—"

"And do what?"

I shrugged helplessly. "I hoped you could guide me, Magister."

Gret said, "There is a priest among the warlocks at Gonlanburg."

I saw nothing strange in that. The Order of Navigators would naturally be interested in the alien girl.

"A Navigator named Peter. Peter of Syrtis. Have you heard of this man?"

It happened that I did, for Peter of Syrtis was the author of a number of shockingly prejudiced books on pre-Imperial solar history. He had earned his name for his habit of making retreats on the barren and almost uninhabitable deserts of Sol's fourth planet. "Earth's wretched sister," he called it. Others called it simply Mars; and it was the home monastery of the Zealots, a subcult among the Navigators dedicated to a return of autocratic clerical power. To the blindly faithful, the Zealots promised paradise. To the heretic, the agnostic, and the freethinker, they held out the whip and the rack and the *auto-da-fé*.

As a historian I knew what a return to the days of the

Grand Inquisitor Talvas would mean to the Empire. As a
man, I shuddered at the thought. The Zealots were few, but
they had friends in high places. And I had been taught to
mistrust bigots. I had no desire to see the scarlet-robed
Inquisitors loose once again in the galaxy.

"That fanatic is at Gonlanburg?" I exclaimed. "I wonder
the warlocks don't pitch him into the sea!"

"He is there as personal emissary of the Grand Master
of Navigators."

"I can't believe it."

"You had better believe it, Starkahn. It is true."

"But Nav Peter is something out of the past. He's a
savage. He's religion gone crazy. Surely we are not to have
a witch-hunt in this day and age?"

"Erit says that Nav Peter is authorized to take the alien
to Algol, to the Theocracy, when the warlocks have revived
her."

"But that's insane, Magister!" I said heatedly. "What will
the Navigators do with her?"

"Our present Grand Master Briffault rules over a diminished Order, Kier. The Navigators have done their part for
civilization, and they are not content now to rest and be
forgotten. I can't answer your question because no one
knows the mind of the high churchmen. But if Peter of
Syrtis is the chosen instrument of the Navigators' policy, I
fear for more than the alien creature's life and well-being."

"The Galacton is removing the alien from our keeping?"

"He would not take her from the Rhad for himself," Gret
said, wearily wise to the ways of men. "But who could
object to her being given into the keeping of the clergy?"

"I wouldn't believe it of Sokolovsky," I exclaimed angrily. "He was a Fleet commander, soldier of the Empire,
before he became a politician— Would he give up the girl
while that hell ship is still loose in the Empire?"

"He would and he will. You touched the truth yourself
just now when you called Sokolovsky a politician. To be
Galacton is, *a priori,* to be a politician, and expedient.

Above all, expedient. Our Galacton was once Elector of Bellatrix, Kier. He knows the way of the mob. And the mob wants no part of a doomsday machine in their midst—not even a single alien girl from it."

"But turning the girl over to the Zealots isn't going to make that black horror go away," I protested. "She is the key to the black starship, and without her there is no chance of our controlling it."

"That's so. But Sokolovsky and the Zealots as well are convinced that the law of averages is against a blind strike hitting an inhabited star system," Gret said.

"But that's crazy! That thing isn't programmed to attack stars at random. It couldn't be. It wouldn't make any sense at all."

"Correct, my young pupil," Gret said. "I have an idea of what logic, if any, the craft is going to follow. But I cannot be sure. There is much to search out before I can guess. One thing, however, must be done at once." The small, naked figure stirred in the gel and, for the first time, spoke aloud: "Erit must be allowed to work with the alien alone. So that this will be possible, when the warlocks wake the girl, you must steal her, Starkahn."

I stood openmouthed, not crediting the evidence of my ears.

"Do you think there is any other way?" Gret asked.

"I—why—I didn't think—" I shook my head. "I don't know, Magister."

"It must be done. At the risk of making you into an even bigger hero to the Royalists—it must be done," Gret said. "The warlocks will attempt the revivification very soon. Since you are not a medic, there is no way we can arrange for you to be present. How even I sometimes yearn for the old times, Kier! Two hundred years ago there would have been no one to prevent your doing whatever you pleased. But then, two hundred years ago no Zealot would have dared set foot in a Rhadan city, let alone our university center. In any case, Kier, the alien must not reach Syrtis—"

"Mars? I thought Nav Peter was under orders to take her to Algol?"

"Perhaps so. But I would wager my life—what is left of it—on the fact that Peter the Zealot would take her to Syrtis Major and not to the Grand Master in Algol. He sees himself as another pope, I think. Perhaps as Pope and Galacton as well. Think of that, Kier. If he has luck, he could do it. And we would all bow head and knee to a Navigator's tyranny while we wait for that black monster to snuff out our suns, one by one—"

"Can Erit reach Ariane?"

A thin smile touched the lips of the creature in the gel. "It has been done. Remember they are both women, and females are schemers at heart." His love for Erit was like a tangible aura in the chamber.

I picked up the Vulk's ancient lyre and brushed my fingertips across the strings, remembering that Gret had taught me to play it himself, as he had taught me many things. No, there would be no return to the Dark Time if I could prevent it.

"I'll be off-world by tonight," I said.

"Yes," Gret said sibilantly. He sounded suddenly tired, worn out by his talk with me. "Yes, it is what you will do," he said. "You are the Rebel's descendant, I am content." And then, relaxing almost into slumber, I felt his control loosen. He was dreaming, in that waking-dream state of the old of every breed and kind. And I saw him—I *rode* with him—through the gates of Nyor while the war mares chanted. I saw the ancient starships rising from the Gonlan Sea and the mounted warbands riding through the forests and mountains with star kings and Navigators at their heads. I even caught a glimpse of the greatest king, Glamiss the Magnificent, who came down from Vyka in the northern galactic wasteland to Earth, raising again the flags and banners over Nyor, Mistress of the Skies—

"I am dreaming, Starkahn," Gret whispered. "What a great thing is history—how beautiful and terrible is the past—"

And with that thought echoing in my mind, I put the lyre carefully down by the tank and went quietly from the room to steal a silver-eyed girl.

Chapter Six

And sin said to man, "Make you Cyb in your image, after your likeness: and give him dominion over the fish of the sea, and over the fowl of the air, and over the cattle, and over every creeping thing that creepeth upon the Earth—I, sin, command this, that man's days may be numbered."

From *The Book of Warls*,
Interregnal period.

And WHEREAS: Cybernetic Organisms have a long tradition of service to the Empire and to mankind; and WHEREAS: Certain vital works of the Empire and man could not be accomplished without the skill, goodwill, and courage of the aforementioned Cybernetic Organisms; Let it THEREFORE BE RESOLVED

*by the SENATE and GENERAL ASSEMBLY of THE
EMPIRE, that Cybernetic Organisms ARE, now and
for all time, CITIZENS of THE EMPIRE and entitled
to all the PRIVILEGES and subject to all the DUTIES
AND RESPONSIBILITIES thereto pertaining....*

Excerpt from the *Galactic Rescript* of 7000 GE,
late Second Stellar Empire period

"Remember, Starkahn, that I, too, am a citizen of the Empire," Ariane said positively. "I leave it to your sense of fair play to assign me a suitable role in the upcoming fiasco."

She had extended her drogue through the airlock into my apartment in the Coral Sands Hostel. The rest of her vast bulk floated in neutral buoyancy outside my room two hundred meters from the sea bottom and twice that from the surface of Zodiac Bay.

Gonlan's mascons are grouped near the polar regions, so gravity is slightly lower than the equator, where the best diving is to be found. Zodiac Bay, an inlet of the Gonlan Sea, is a basin of fine blue water alive with fish and the varied sea mammals of Gonlan. The Coral Sands Hostel is a favorite vacation place for tourists from the galactic center and for Rim-born personnel of the Fleet on leave.

ADSPS cyborgs, in particular, like to spend their leaves in Zodiac Bay playing manta. Their shape predisposes them to the sea, of course. And at Zodiac Bay the human members of the survey teams can obtain cryogenic rebreather implants so that they can disport themselves with their cyborgs at any depth down to seven hundred meters. The psychologists tell us that there is something soothing about a return to the sea, this being apparently true for both man and cyb, who after all was made, as the *Warls* tell us, in man's image.

So I was resting in my sea quarters: a room built of corals, damp and smelling deliciously of sea. I say deliciously because my implanted "lung" relished the salty moisture of the air and the pelagic flavor that permeated every part of the vast coral warren. And as I rested from the trip from Rhada and from the sea trip aboard the hovercraft to the marker buoy and then the deep dive to the hostel, I listened to Ariane tell me what she had learned from Erit of what was happening in the laboratories of the University of Gonlanburg.

I said, "You don't have to remind me that you are a citizen, Ariane. I suggested only that it might be better if you stayed out of the misdemeanor I'm planning. Even a cyborg can be reprogrammed if the offense is great enough."

"You're risking it." Ariane spoke reproachfully. "Should I do less? I thought we were friends."

"We are," I said. "And don't get bristly with me and start quoting me chapter and verse about your civil rights. I know the law as well as you do. That's the problem. You've already involved yourself in too much. Before we've done, I may be in front of a court martial or even an ecclesiatical synod. We haven't had a heresy trial in the Empire for a thousand years, but this just might be the time. You've heard of Peter of Syrtis."

"Peter the Hermit. Peter the Idiot. I know all about him," Ariane said. "A fanatic. He can't possibly give us trouble."

"He's the Grand Master's personal nuncio to Gonlanburg. The warlords will treat him very carefully indeed. He has the Galacton's authority, as well."

"All the more reason for me to get into this. How did you plan to get off-world with the girl? Even assuming you could get to her and get her away from the university?"

"I hadn't thought of that yet," I said.

"Ah, Kier. What would you do without me—or Lady Nora—or someone to look out for you?" Ariane asked, womanlike. I could feel the coral tremble as she moved her fifteen metric tons restlessly outside the tower. A lovely swirl of bubbles and fishes stormed past the windows in the blue-green sea light.

"Ariane," I said. "All my earlier objections still stand. It is my responsibility. Gret agrees with that, by the way. The alien is the key to the starship. There will be no controlling the ship without the girl. But—"

"No buts. You cannot succeed without me. Ergo, I must

participate. What is our program?"

"Where is Erit?"

"At Gonlanburg. She will contact me when the alien is revived. I should say—*if.*"

I thought about the beautiful girl floating in the life-support capsule and decided that I wanted very much for the warlocks to revive her. And only a part of my hope was concerned with our chances of catching up with—and neutralizing—her deadly doomsday machine.

"The Gonlani-Rhad warlocks are the best on the Rim," I said. "If the thing can be done—if there is any scientific hope—then it *will* be done."

"So Erit says," Ariane murmured. "But what then, Starkahn? How do we spirit an alien being out of the laboratories? And what do we do with her then?"

"The last part I can answer right away. We take her to Gret. He and Erit can put her in Triad. At least the mystery will be solved. What happens next is anybody's guess. Lady Nora wants to use this incident, as she calls it, to build support for the Rhandon royalists. . . ."

"I am deeply attached to you and to Lady Nora as well," Ariane said severely. "But I don't approve of royalist plots. It's archaic to think of bringing back the Rhadan monarchy."

I smiled ruefully at that, though I couldn't have agreed with her more. "Well, no matter. We'll face that problem when the time is right for it," I said. "The important thing is being ready to take the alien the moment the warlocks bring her around. We can't wait. Not only might Nav Peter take her off to Algol or Mars or somewhere—we don't know what *her* powers may be. We will have to take her before she regains all her faculties."

"What a man creature you really are, Kier," Ariane said in a disapproving tone. "I would never have thought about that."

I wanted to leave the hostel at once and penetrate the university grounds. I could do that because of my reputation as an amateur historian and because I was the Starkahn. But Ariane would have none of it. Erit was watching the warlocks, and she would say when we should move. Meanwhile, Ariane declared, it was important that she and I should appear to be nothing more than a human-cyborg survey team on holiday, diving in the crystalline waters of the Gonlan Sea.

The Coral Sands Hostel was one of a cluster of tourist accommodations on the main reef of Zodiac Bay. The guest chambers honeycombed the reef, and the public rooms, wet and dry, were extensive and quite luxurious for the Rim.

There were perhaps eight hundred to a thousand guests at Zodiac Bay, and of this number more than half were unattached women from every nation of the Empire. For some reason it is traditional in our time for women from the galactic center to flock to the Rim, hoping to find marriageable males. Group marriages have become very much the thing in the Inner Nations, and there are always women who seek the more old-fashioned morality of the Rim, where one husband to one wife is still the general rule.

But the girls at the Coral Reef soon identified me as an SW officer vacationing with my cyborg, and consequently they pointedly avoided me. Women who lead approximately normal lives seldom can understand the relationship between a man and a cyborg and soon conclude that the man (mentally addled by long periods in deep space, probably) is in love with (or at least infatuated with) a fifteen-ton creature of metal and tissue resembling a giant devilfish. The result is not conducive to easy relationships between SW pilots and women seeking husbands or lovers.

On our third morning of diving together, I headed for the sea-lock and a swim in company with Ariane. As I swam out to meet her, the clean, vaguely salty seawater flowed through the gills of my implant. The light at this depth was mostly blue-green, and shoals of firefish darted brilliantly across the shimmering coral of the reef. My worries about Gonlanburg and what I must do there were fading in the beauty of the sea. The nitrogen content of the Gonlan Sea is low, but at a depth of more than two hundred meters, the effect of the gas concentration is slightly euphoric. This "rapture of the depths" was once a serious problem to divers on all the water planets. But, with the discovery of the cryogenic rebreathing implants—the "gills"—that permit air-breathing mammals to breathe water at ambient pressure, any damage from the "rapture" almost vanished. Today it is a relaxing phenomenon more popular than alcohol or drugs.

In the sapphire distance I could make out Ariane's manta form. She was swinging slowly about in circles, waiting for me. Quite suddenly I was reminded of the way she looked in deep space, with the light of the now murdered Delphinus star on her, and I wasn't so euphoric any more.

But Ariane was a pleasant sight, silently gliding through the deep, clear water at swimming pace. The cyborg, who could move in the void at speeds that were multiples of the velocity of light, was swimming lazily, spiraling down, rolling, hanging weightless in the abyss, all with the grace of a ballet dancer.

The waters of the Gonlan Sea near Zodiac Bay are reasonably warm, but there are some deep trenches in the sea bottom off the continental shelf, so that there are many currents of much colder water flowing through the bay. These can be seen as streaks of murky green, rivers of dull color flowing through the cobalt and sapphire depths.

Ariane would penetrate one of these green torrents and slip into the lower abyss, into areas of pressure far too great for a man, even one equipped with gills. For a time she would vanish, and then she would come jetting up through the warmer layers, her sleek flanks roiling the water in shock waves so that she seemed wreathed in silver.

Pressing the base of my skull against the encephalophone pickup, I subvocalized, calling Ariane across the intervening sea. "Very pretty. Now slow down and let me join you."

"Come along," Ariane said. "Do you want to ride or swim?"

I kicked closer to her with my jet fins, enjoying the silky feel of the cool sea on my skin through my sea suit. "I'll swim, thanks. We may not have much chance to do this again later on."

Ariane coasted slowly through the blue water, with me swimming just over her titanium prow, for all the world like the remora fish of the terrestrial ocean.

"Have you heard from Erit?" I asked, after a lazy interval.

"Wait until we are farther from the reef. The Navigators have been known to monitor short-range encephalophone conversations."

We swam in silence out into the center of the bay until we were englobed by empty water, miles of it, free even of fishes, which disliked the frigid waters rising from the deepsea trenches.

"You had better come aboard," Ariane said. "I don't want to discuss this on external circuits."

I was reluctant to leave the sea: carrying an implanted gill creates a psychological dependence on the ocean—the great mother of life and all that. But Ariane opened the airlock invitingly, and I moved a bit up the evolutionary scale and came aboard to stand, dripping, in the lock as she pumped the water back into the sea.

I hadn't been aboard Ariane since returning from our last ill-fated deep space probe, and she had been partially refitted since then. I was soon to discover why, and it came as a real shock to me. But for the moment I merely stood, shivering a little at the air on my skin and gasping a little as the medium in my lungs changed from water to Ariane's oxygen-rich gas mixture. I felt a little heady as the stuff speeded up my metabolism. I stepped from the lock into Ariane's bridge. I kicked away my fins, but with the tubing of the cryogenic gill still protruding from my chest, I felt a bit like a cyborg myself.

I sank down onto the familiar comfort of the acceleration couch and— Only, somehow, it wasn't quite as comfortable as it should have been. The contours were wrong, unfamiliar. I didn't like it. It was a surprise in circumstances where there should have been nothing but the deliciously comforting touch of the *accustomed*.

Ariane's voice came clearly to me: "So you've noticed."

"What have the refitters done here?" I demanded.

"Those aren't your measurements in the control couch, are they?"

"No. Definitely not." I felt angry and cheated, somehow. No one had the right to make changes like this. The relationship between SW team pairs was so close, so unique, that unauthorized modifications were like interference between a man and wife—and on the most intimate level.

"I couldn't be sure before," Ariane said. "I had no way to measure the changes they made during the refit."

"You couldn't be sure of what?" I asked.

"Did the Court of Inquiry release *all* of its findings?" she asked.

"They announced the reprimand in the All Fleets," I said.

"Well, they wouldn't mention a change of assignment until it was actually made, would they?" she said.

I was dense enough to fail to understand her.

"Look around you," Ariane said. "Any other changes?"

I did as she told me and moved about the tiny bridge with increasing consternation. "My reading tapes are gone. So are all the rest of my personal belongings. What's the meaning of this, Ariane? Why didn't you say something to me?"

"I wasn't sure," she said. "After all, if a surgeon went to work on *you*, could you say for sure what he took out?"

The accuracy of that homey analogy was beyond my disputing.

"The Bureau of Personnel is going to break us up," I said, aghast. Not that the military gods and goddesses lacked the right and authority to change our assignments. That was unquestioned. But it was a thing almost never done; unheard of in the Fleet, actually. SW teams were, by custom, sacrosanct. Then *why* were Ariane and I being reclassified?

"It is something to think about, isn't it, Kier," she said. "We come back from a probe with the first specimen of what could be a lost branch of *homo sapiens,* with news of a doomsday machine loose in the galaxy—and what happens? You are nearly court-martialed, and I'm sent off to play in the sea, and neither of us are told that we are being reassigned. Now who had the power to do something like that, Starkahn? Tell me who?"

I threw myself disconsolately onto the now-ill-fitting contour couch and said, *"You tell me,* Ariane—"

"I can't. This is human behavior. No cyborg ever behaved so sneakily. I can't help you. But I can guess that it was someone who wants no further investigation of the black starship or, quite possibly, the girl in the support capsule."

"But that's absurd, Ariane. To do something like this, a person would have to have tremendous influence in Imperial circles—among high officers of the Fleet at Nyor. And he—or she—would have to be almost paranoiac about investigating spatio-historical probabilities..." My voice trailed off into uncertainty because it sounded vaguely as though I were describing someone I'd heard about recently—an influential fanatic.

"I know what you are thinking," Ariane said. "But there is another possibility."

"There are dozens of possibilities," I said irritably. "Maybe hundreds. Its just that we don't know about any of them. We are only guessing."

"Nav Peter of Syrtis," Ariane said. "Or Lady Nora."

I grew really angry at that: Ariane grouping the fanatic Navigator with my mother.

"Think about it," Ariane said. "An Inquisitor a few thousand years out of his time and yearning for the good old days could do something like this. *We* found the alien, after all. The black starship could be the scourge of God, the sword of the holy Star, in his mind. You name it. Your history is filled with that kind of thinking. And when you are a fanatic, you don't investigate growing legends—you *encourage* them.... They are the way to power. And remember—the Fleet can send out a hundred cruisers—but the only ones with any real chance of locating the black ship again are you and me. There is one possibility. Has the monk enough influence with the Galacton to pull the right wires and separate us?"

"He might well have," I said, still angry. "But that's only your first guess. What about Lady Nora?"

"That is a different matter," Ariane said. "We both know her. We both know her ambitions for you. She could put up with our relationship to one another as long as you were just a frustrated historian—yes, it's so, and there is no denying it, so don't try. I have the greatest admiration for the Lady Nora Veg-Rhad, and we have a great many things in common. Our wishes for you, for example. But *she* wants to bring back the past on Rhada. She wants to build a great, antique social pyramid and put you, the Starkahn, on the top of it. Now that you are a hero to the Rhada, a source of concern to the Imperials and the clergy, too, I wouldn't be surprised, why the thing to do is obvious. Make dead certain you stay on Rhada to play politics. How better to do that than pull some strings and have one of her friends in the Fleet—that lady admiral, for example—arrange a discreet shuffle of computer cards in Bu Personnel?"

"She wouldn't do that," I protested. But, of course, I knew that she would. And she would with only the best will in the world. My Lady Mother, sad to relate, would happily dismantle my entire life and career to serve some mystical sense of *noblesse* and family ambition. Ariane knew it, and so did I.

"That is why," the cyborg said matter-of-factly, "I have no intention of returning to the Fleet base at New Kynan when my leave is up. At least not until we've delivered that silver-eyed creature to Gret-Erit and found her ghastly machine as well."

I assimiliated that with difficulty. There has not been an authenticated case of mutiny in the Fleet since the Interregnum, and I was about to start reading the *Articles for the Governance of the Fleet* to Ariane when I realized that she was absolutely right and functioning with direct cyborg honesty and logic. The threat of random destruction of stellar systems had to be met with intelligence, not with greater force—for there *was* no greater force, not in any nation that we knew, nearby or across the spiral arms of the galaxy.

"All right," I said finally. "When do we begin our short happy careers as mutineers?" Before she replied, I knew the answer.

"Erit is waiting for us in Gonlanburg *now*," Ariane said.

"So my question is academic?" I said, half resentfully.

"The decision is really yours to make, Kier," Ariane said.

"They have revived the alien?"

"This morning. So Erit says."

I didn't ask how Ariane knew. If she said she did, then she knew. It came as no surprise that there could be a telepathic bond between Vulk and cyborg. Both of their minds were, in that sense, more highly developed than man's.

"Then," I said, "I suppose the time *is* now."

"Yes," Ariane said, and I felt her leap from the darkness of the sea.

Chapter Seven

Kier, the king, and Ariane, the silver princess,
Rode the night wind, and in their hands were truth
swords,
And righteousness mantled their shoulders,
And honor was in their heads—
Yet the way was difficult. So it is.
Even for heroes.

Guest Song, authorship unknown,
early Second Stellar Empire period

Wjen Ey be dead And long forgotten, then lyt it be
Syd of me that Ey dyd my duty to My People; wielding
in Thyr Name thye myghtiest Engines and Weapons
of destruction thyt Men hyve yyt Conceived and using
thyr own Scyence that thyye have corrupted for the

Banishment of all that is best and Fynest among Thye People....

> Oath administered to Watchers of each
> of the three *Deaths* before their departure
> from the Communes of Magellan.
> Engraving found on the bulkhead
> wreckage of *Death Two*
> during the early Confederate period

So I came back to Gonlanburg: a naked man with the tubes of an artificial gill still jutting from my chest, aboard a cyborg ship already allotted to some other Survey pilot.

The change in assignments, Ariane and I surmised, was not yet official, so there was no immediate problem about our whereabouts and whether or not we were together. Thus it was possible for her to remain quite openly at the civil spaceport while I, playing the bookish Starkahn, had a haberdasher come aboard to outfit me in a tunic and kilt of the sort worn by students at the university. I bought a wig from the man, too, so that I could wear the encephalophone contacts on my mastoid bones without causing too much curiosity among the school people. Long hair is far more common in the colleges of the Rim than are bits of SW equipment such as E-phones.

It was nearly evening when I was finally ready to leave the port and go searching for Erit in the university gardens. Ariane's presence in the civil docking area was causing more of a stir than either of us thought safe or suitable: the merchant fleets have nothing comparable to the ADSPS cyborgs. It was only a matter of time until someone, the Lady Nora perhaps, or the Fleet authorities, or even some misguided Navigator working for the Zealots, would locate us and become interested in what it was brought us to the same city as the alien we had discovered in Delphinus. So we filed a flight plan for Ariane back to Rhada, and as I left the port in a rented hovercraft, I caught a glimpse of Ariane's manta silhouette rising above the jumble of gantries, hangars, and veetols docked in the port.

We had deliberately filed for a free-fall course out to Gonlan-Omicron's orbit, and then translight to the Rhada sun. This would leave Ariane unreported for the better part of eleven hours—which was enough time for her to establish herself in synchronous orbit directly over Gonlanburg and wait for my E-phone call. She could act as commo satellite between me and Erit, as well, if conditions for Vulk-to-cyborg telepathy were good.

Filing a false flight plan was a reprogramming offense for both Ariane and for me, but it seemed that the more deeply we involved ourselves in the recovery of the alien girl, the more we found ourselves in conflict with the establishment and the law. I am not, as my famous ancestor was, a rebel by nature. But when every instinct warns me that the powers-that-be are handling something important in a rash and ill-considered way, then I will take personal action. I am, after all, the Starkahn and a Rhad. I explained many transgressions that way in my lifetime. But I had a feeling that if things went badly now, the explanation wouldn't save me.

Yet there was something else to consider, as a mental discipline only, because it is quite impossible for a man— one single man—to come to terms, *actual* terms, with the destruction of whole solar systems. As a soldier, one might readily understand the sort of death and havoc created by a laser rifle, or even nuclear torpedo. But carnage on a planetary scale, let alone on a stellar one, is simply impossible to conceive, except as an abstract notion. I personally had witnessed the destruction of the Delphinus star, yet I had no genuine grasp of the meaning of such power, such genocide plus. Nor, I suspected, did the unknowns who constructed the black starship. By such minds were pogroms launched and epidemics started in the murk of human history.

I was certain that no single human being could come to working terms with the meaning of a real doomsday machine. What did that leave, then, as the markers of it? True aliens? I thought of the girl's silver eyes and wondered if that were her only "difference." Or the mass hysteria of some rabid human organization so maddened with self-amplifying hate that it would contrive the random death of stars—and in so doing consign to glowing plasma billions of living things?

The result of this soul-searching was to make it crystal clear that my potential personal troubles were academic. If the black starship came to Rhadan space (and why should it not?), then the local authorities, the Rhadan units of the Fleet, a few hundred civilian starships, Gret, Erit, my mother, the alien girl, Ariane, the faculty warlocks of Gonlanburg, Nav Peter the Fanatic, the Rhadan Royalists *(and* the Rhadan Republicans, Collectivists, Anarchists, Disciplinarians, and so on), this city and all the other cities in Rhada, together with Sublieutenant the Honorable Kier Kynan Emeric Veg-Rhad, Starkahn of Rhada, would be superheated molecules of gas in free space, driven into the intergalactic void by light-pressure from a swollen and dying star. *That* much, I *knew.* The knowledge didn't allow much room for maneuver.

Gonlanburg is an old town; some of its buildings date back to Interregnal times, and in the years since then it has been relatively untouched by wars. The other towns and cities of Gonlan, the inland agricultural centers and the industrial complexes along the northern coast, are relatively modern (on Gonlan that means they were founded within the last millennium), and they have all been shattered at least once by armies or air forces. But even in the process of taking Gonlan from the Interregnal kings, the warmen of my family treated Gonlanburg kindly. Perhaps it is because the place stirs racial memories of old university towns on Earth, towns that exist no longer save in the memory of men.

Gonlanburg has been a seat of learning time out of

mind. In the days of Kynan the Navigator, who was Star King of the Gonlani-Rhad during the reign of the Galacton Torquas the Poet, in the second century of the sixth millennium GE, the Gonlani warlocks conducted their researches in secret, hiding their rediscoveries of the old knowledge from the members of the holy Order of Navigators. Much of the early work on cyborg rebirth and organ transplantation was done in those days by the warlocks of Gonlanburg.

It had been some years since I had traveled through the narrow, rose-stone streets of Gonlanburg, and anxious as I was, a part of me was enjoying it. It was dusk, a quiet time in the old university town. The shops were closing down, storekeepers covering their wares with the silver nets they had used in this place to prevent theft for a thousand years. There were students on the streets, as well, more boys than girls (because we are still traditionalists out here on the Rim and do not encourage women to take up intellectual pursuits), but yet some girls (we aren't barbarians, after all), pretty ones in their student kilts and tunics. Some of the young people carried Vulkish musical instruments, for Gonlanburg is a galactic center of the study of Vulk music and art.

The students mingled with the townspeople, throngs of them in a bright-colored river of shimmering caps and capes and cloaks. The people of the Rim, perhaps because of the loneliness of their almost empty sky, are lovers of color and light. The old stone buildings blazed with flurons, colored electrics, even with flame sconces, fed by the blue-burning gases piped from far inland. The occasional aluminum and quartz building erected in the last century or so glittered amid the red stones of the ancient town.

I drove the hovercraft slowly toward the university gardens, in some places stalled by the traffic of hovers, carts, three-wheelers, electrics, and animal-drawn wagons. The Gonlani-Rhad, having been brought into the Palatinate late, were of course more Rhad than the Rhad of Rhada. There were now more Rhadan war horses and mares on Gonlan than on any other world in the Rhadan Republic. Even here on the crowded, dusky streets of Gonlanburg, I could see many riders on their fine specimens—horses, but with a difference: clawed fighting feet and the pads of cats, carniverous teeth and slotted eyes, and—most unusual of all to the stranger from the central galaxy—no reins or head gear, for these animals were telepathic, with a rudimentary language and culture.

For hundreds of generations the Rhad had bred these splendid animals: once for war, now for show and pleasure. Some said the original stock had been brought in sperm banks from Earth in the time of the First Empire. It might well be so, though there are no Rhadan horses on Earth now save those imported for the Imperial court from Rhada.

The newsfax telexes on the building cornices carried the ordinary run of news from throughout the Empire. There was not a single word about the doomsday machine, nor about anything untoward happening anywhere within the inhabited galaxy. I wondered if the destruction of Sigma Libra and the Delphinus star was being suppressed—or was it simply that the spread of man throughout the galaxy was so enormous, so sprawling-huge, that the destruction of two small stars out of billions could not force itself through the inertia of workaday news? Either way it was dangerous and frightening, because the threat was real and the death it promised swift and sure.

I turned away from the commercial districts and fed power to the hover jets, hurrying toward the acropolis where the university stood. As I guided the machine up the winding path, I felt the tingle of an encephalophone transmission coming from a great distance.

I pressed the powerstud against my skull under the wig, and Ariane immediately began to speak impatiently to me.

"I've been calling you for almost a half hour," she said crossly.

"I was in traffic. Too much interference at this range, I guess."

"I am sychronized. Eleven hundred sixty-five point four kilometers."

"Good."

"Erit is waiting for you now in the eucalyptus garden of the science faculty. You know where that is?"

"Yes," I said. "I have been here before."

"Apologies, Starkahn." Ariane could pick the damnedest times to get snippish and feminine with me. But perhaps her position, in an illegal orbit eleven hundred kilometers over my head, had something to do with her state of mind. Being a cyborg, Ariane was by nature a law-abiding creature. All this carrying on was really against her normal inclinations.

"Erit has arranged for the two of you to see the alien. She has told the warlocks you are a student of hers from Rhada, a xenobiologist. If they don't recognize you, it should come off."

"And if they do?"

"Why, then, you will have to think of something very quickly, Starkahn."

I should have known that would be her reply. Even in these circumstances, Ariane couldn't help schooling me. The psychometrists who teamed us must have built a "throw him out of the nest" syndrome into our relationship.

At the base of the acropolis, I left the hovercraft in a copse of thornbushes. There were no students on the paths at this time of evening. Those who were attending or leaving classes in the clinical departments above would be using the less scenic, but much more efficient, pneumatic tunnels inside the basalt structure of the hill.

I was some hundred meters now above the level of the town of Gonlanburg proper, and from here I could see the polychromatic spread of the lights of city and spaceport. The port boundaries were outlined in violet high-visibility fluoros, and beyond them lay the restless darkness of the Gonlan Sea. Far down the coast, at Zodiac Bay, the water would be lighted with the firefly glow of hundreds of night divers and the brightness of the underwater hostels like the

Coral Sands and the others on the reef.

But here, in these northern waters, no such tourist attractions existed. The sea was cold off Gonlanburg and very deep. The darkness beyond the starship port was as vast and lonely as the sky above it: an emptiness lit only by the dim outline of the galactic lens and the faint, distant luminosity of the Magellanic Clouds, a long lifetime away, even at translight velocities.

I hurried up the steeply climbing path toward the garden of the science faculty. The night wind made a sighing sound in the unseen eucalyptus trees: those hundred-meter giants imported long ago from Earth to thrive in Gonlan's bright sun and sea airs. But I could not see the trees, for Gonlan's sky at night is dark. The nearest stars are few, and the satellites, Alpha through Omicron, are no more than half a kilometer in diameter. They dart across the sky like meteors but shed no real light on the surface of the planet.

At the top of the hill, where the path leveled and entered the grove, I stopped. I could hear voices ahead in the darkness, and I had no way of knowing if they were the voices of someone I wanted to avoid or merely students making out in the privacy of the orderly forest.

Two cowled shapes materialized out of the darkness, and I realized that they were two Navigators, young novices by their voices, and apparently members of the retinue of Nav Peter of Syrtis. Their conversation was about what one would expect of two young men suddenly thrust into the student society of Gonlanburg. Navigators are not celibates, though they live in a largely male world. And Gonlanburg's female students, while not numerous, were Rim women and more than customarily handsome.

I leaned against a large tree and listened with some sense of tolerant superiority. After all, it was *my* people they were discussing. But then one said: "Still, I've seen nothing to match the silver-eyed goddess."

"Nor has Nav Peter," his friend replied in an awed voice. "I've never seen him so incensed."

"She spat on him and called him 'Genie.' Why would she do such a thing? Could there be Navigators where she came from?"

"That doesn't make any sense. Think how long she has been in that capsule, and now—"

Their voices faded, and I could hear no more, nor did I think it wise to follow them to spy on their conversation. Erit, if I could find her in this darkness, would answer the questions as they arose. Yet the young priests seemed to be saying that Nav Peter was already angry, already hostile to the alien. Gret's suggestion that the Zealot clergyman might take the alien off to Syrtis rather than to Algol as his superiors ordered became more of a possibility.

I pressed the power stud on the E-phone and called out to Ariane. The reply was slow and indistinct. The planet's ionization layer was interfering capriciously. "Where is Erit now?" I asked.

"Here beside you," a voice said in the blackness, startling me.

"Erit," I said, feeling the sudden warmth of her presence. "Thank the Star you're here."

Now I could make out the small humanoid shape: a duplicate in almost every way of Gret, yet somehow unmistakably "female," or at least different in some sexual sense from Gret's "maleness." She stirred in the darkness and touched my arm. Immediately, my sense of well-being grew.

"They revived the girl this morning," Erit said. "They have not questioned her yet. She is still too weak. But Nav Peter saw her."

"I heard two of his novices talking," I said. "There was some sort of trouble."

"She grew very agitated. She called him a 'Genie' among other things—none of them very complimentary. The girl speaks almost perfect Anglic."

The language of the Golden Age, I thought. I had never heard it used. My head spun with the implications of what

Erit said. The alien girl must be a living mine of historical
data. Was it really possible she had been in that support
capsule since First Empire times? And what could she mean
by calling a Navigator a 'Genie'? Was it possible she had
never before *seen* a member of the Order? If that were so,
then she must actually be as ancient in origin as I supposed.
The Order of Navigators was formed in Interregnal times,
after the First Empire, to protect and maintain the starships.

"She is sleeping now," Erit said in the darkenss. "This
afternoon she was given a hypnocourse in *lingua spacia*.
The warlocks decided that would be simpler than trying to
locate someone fluent enough in Anglic to converse with
her." She stirred restlessly, and I could feel, quite suddenly,
her anxiety to be done with this business and away—back
to Gret. And together with her anxiety came the knowledge
that she might soon be alone, and the loneliness was a
physical ache in the heart.

I said, "You will always have a home among the Rhad,
Erit." It was a blunt and perhaps insensitive thing to say,
and this was a poor time to say it. But I wanted her to know
that my family and I acknowledged our debt to her in per-
petuity. Gret was very old and would surely die one day—
it might be very soon. Certainly Erit felt this, for this was
the source of her anxiety and wish to have done with all
this—and when it happened, Erit, who had been sister-wife
and alter ego to Gret, would be *alone* as no human being
could conceive of being alone. Yet she must know that the
place filled by Gret for so long among the Rhad of Rhada
was hers—for as many more millennia as she lived. Such
knowledge could not assuage the grief that was coming to
the Vulk, but it might make the loneliness easier to bear.

"I know this, Starkahn," Erit said. "But it is kind of you
to understand my anxiousness to be back with him."

"Tonight, Erit," I said. "We will start this very night."

"Perhaps, Starkahn."

"We will take the girl now," I said, with a confidence I
didn't completely feel.

"I will guide you to her," Erit said, starting up the path.

At the crest of the hill we came out of the dark into the glow of the gardens of the clinical wing. There were patients walking on the terraces and some few warlocks, their traditional black robes marking them among the white-clothed inmates of the hospital.

They made formal greeting to Erit as she led me along the corridors to the isolation wing. I looked for armed guards. Surely, I thought, the Imperials would have so important a "detainee" under some guard. But all I could see were a few young Navigators, none of them obviously armed, except for the traditional flintlock pistols at their belts.

We descended a shallow ramp into a rotunda where a group of warlocks stood in conversation before the door to a suite. The warlocks were all medical doctors by their scarlet collars, and as Erit approached, they bowed and looked curiously at me.

"This is Emeric, Doctors. A student of mine from Rhada. I have promised him a moment with our patient," Erit said.

"Of a certainty, Clarissima," the eldest warlock replied. No warlock would refuse so reasonable a request by a Vulk— not in a Rim nation, and most particularly not on any planet of the Rhadan Republic, where Gret and Erit were known and revered by all classes.

The doctors still regarded me with some puzzlement, but they were too polite to ask questions.

"Shall we come with you, Clarissima?" the warlock asked. "The observation chamber is open. The alien girl is asleep."

"Thank you, we can manage," Erit murmured, and led on through a series of doors. In the third inner chamber robots produced sterile gowns and respirators. The hospital was taking no chances with alien bacteria, though Erit assured me the girl was quite safe and free of infection of any sort.

I said, "Have Ariane send a drone now. Do you know which window is the alien's?"

"Yes," Erit said.

I felt the harmonics of the Vulk's strong telepathic transmission. It was beamed narrowly to Ariane's cyborg wavelength, but the overload charged the room and set the primitive colloidal brains of service robots to stirring. Their utilitarian appendages twitched with the strength of impulses they were too incomplete to interpret and translate action.

"The drone is launched, Starkahn," Erit said.

"It will cause quite a stir in the town, you know," I said. "And there will be Fleet personnel at the port who will be able to figure out what it is. But not immediately, I hope." I shrugged. "I'm sorry, in any case. It was the best plan I could devise. The only one, in fact."

"It will do," Erit said. "If we do our part."

And, I thought, *if no one interferes!* Our plan was so lightly cobbled together, using what resources we could muster, that a single unforeseen factor could ruin us.

I stood finally in the last sterile chamber, the sterile drapes over my cavalier's wig, tunic, and kilt.

"She is there," Erit said, indicating the massive steel and plastic door ahead of us.

"All right," I said. My heart was pounding, and I did not know with any degree of certainty whether what I felt was anxiety or suppressed pleasure at the thought of seeing that beautiful woman again.

Chapter Eight

The male members of the house of Rhada were, since earliest times, strong warriors and enlightened (if severe) rulers. They were also, one is constrained to say, highly susceptible to women. This, one supposes, is a malady of kings.

> Einar Baltus-Yoka WL.D.,
> *The Evolution of the Rhadan Republic,*
> late Second Stellar Empire period

If she is, as you suspect, a descendant of transportees, then it may be that she has knowledge that should be restricted to members of the Order.

> Fragment of a letter from Grand Master
> of Navigators Briffault
> to Nav Peter of Syrtis,

Special Nuncio and Inquisitor,
late Second Stellar Empire period

*Yes, there may be danger. But the galaxy and the
Empire are very large—can I not expect peace in my
time?*
   Sokolovsky Bel Ami, Galacton, *Aphorisms,*
   late Second Stellar Empire period

The room in which the alien girl had been revived was a
prison. It was as comfortable as a hospital room can be
made, and it was designed for health and well-being. But
it was conclusively and unmistakably a cell. I could see the
apertures that had been made for laser projectors to be
mounted in the walls and the connections for closed-circuit
holography. Fortunately for my plans, such as they were,
the University of Gonlanburg is no more efficient or competent when dealing with the real world than universities
have been for a thousand years or more. The lasers and
holocameras had not yet been installed because there was
a debate among members of the Humanities Faculty (who
had not yet been cleared to interview the revived alien)
concerning a possible violation of the alien girl's civil rights.
I thanked the humanists most fervently. Without their irritation with the "establishment" of the college, I would never
have been able to extract the girl from Gonlanburg.

Erit and I came through the door, and there were still
two attendants watching us through the one-way glass of
the near wall. Erit froze into concentrated immobility, established a mind-touch, and from that moment on what the
attendants saw took place only in the mind of the Vulk and
not in the room they were supposed to be watching.

But I froze into immobility of a sort as well. I had not
seen the girl since leaving her at the port on my return from
deep space. And then, of course, she had been deep in her
coma, floating in the clear fluid of the life-support capsule.

Now, however, she was alive—unmistakably so. There
were soft movements, a delicate flush on her cheeks, a

tendril of dark hair falling endearingly across her narrow
brow. Her breath was slow and deep in natural sleep. This
was no specimen in a crystal tube. This was a young and
beautiful woman lying with her head on the softly tinted
pillows, her small and delicately made hand on the coun-
terpane. She made my chest ache and my breath come more
quickly: she was altogether beautiful and touching, for, I
reminded myself, had anyone ever been as alone as this
girl? The black starship had brought her across an infinity
of kilometers from some unknown place through years—
eons, probably—of measureless time. And now, even the
vessel was gone, and she, small and beautiful and helpless,
was *alone*.

"Kier," Erit spoke quietly. "I cannot double-track my
mind forever. Hurry, or I shall lose my hold on the attendants."

I started and realized that I has slipped into my old ways:
daydreaming and fantasizing—being the warman-errant of
history, about to rescue a fair lady. In truth, I had to admit
to myself that I wasn't *rescuing* the alien girl. If anything,
what I had in mind was to *kidnap* her, and, with the help
of my Vulkish assistants, to pick her brain.

I used the encephalophone and made contact with Ariane.
She reported that the drone had completed reentry and was
hovering over the security wing of the hospital awaiting my
transmission to localize itself. "Get it started," I ordered.

Within seconds I heard the first faint hissing of a laser
cutting through the wall and the sputtering spark of a short-
circuited alarm system. Then two things happened at once.
The alien girl opened her eyes and looked at me, and Nav
Peter of Syrtis walked through the door into the room.

The girl's silver eyes found me, and the effect was remarkable. The slotted pupils had been dilated so that the
eyes themselves seemed dark and liquid. But as her attention
focused on me, the pupils contracted to slits, the way cat's
eyes will when struck by a strong light. Then her expression,
which had been soft and almost languorous, changed, too,
and she opened her mouth and screamed.

That scream may well have saved my life, for Nav Peter, his shaven skull gleaming in the hard lights and his ceremonial flintlock pistol in his hand, would probably have shot me simply out of surprise at finding me in the alien's chamber. It was the first time I had actually seen the fanatical Navigator, and the sight wasn't reassuring. His face was gray and smooth as polished granite. His eyes were deepset and burning, the eyes of a man who believes he has seen God.

He stared at me and started to ask, *"Who—?"* Then he saw Erit and heard the hissing of the laser from the drone outside the window. Meanwhile, the alien girl had stopped screaming and sat like an image, her expression frozen into one of bewildered, terror-stricken disbelief. I hoped that she had been screaming at the Navigator rather than at me, but it didn't really matter. Either of us could easily have been a source of fright to her. One had to think of whence she had come and how her surroundings must look to her.

But Nav Peter, like all Navigators, was trained to use his mind swiftly and to make quick decisions. He raised the pistol to cover me and went for his communicator as well. It was that extra movement that gave me my single chance. The laser beam was through the wall. There was almost no time at all, certainly no time for a prolonged fight with a fanatical priest. Before he could either shoot or speak into the communicator, I had chopped him down with an openhanded blow on the throat. I had a fleeting thought: to all my other crimes—add sacrilege. It bothered me, but it had to be done. Erit was saying, "My hold on the attendants is failing." That meant that they were probably "seeing" two things at once, like a strange double-image. They saw a peaceful room with the alien girl alone and sleeping, and at the same time they saw what was actually taking place in the room, with the falling Navigator, the girl sitting up in terror, the laser cutting a hole in the outside wall, and the black night showing through. They would start howling an alarm in seconds.

A two-meter section of wall fell in with a sizzle of burning plastic, and I moved swiftly forward to the girl's bedside and said, "Forgive me." I didn't have time for refinements. I rapped her sharply across the chin, and she slumped delicately into my arms. I shouted to Erit for her to *go*, and she slipped swiftly through the wall and onto the smooth, curving back of the drone that hung in null-grav against the outside wall of the hospital building. Below, in the garden, there was some commotion as passersby began peering up into the darkness at the confusion outside the hospital wall.

I wrapped a blanket around the girl. Not much help there, because it was a power blanket and about as heavy as spiderwebs—quite useless out of range of the power projector in the hospital building. Still, I had to wrap her in something. The hospital gown could hardly be called a gown at all, reaching, as it did, approximately to the sternum. Then I gathered her up and went through the wall after Erit, squeezing every volt of energy out of the E-phone and shouting for Ariane to start the drone away.

Through the melted wall I could see the fallen Navigator stirring. He was tough as leather. The chop I gave him would have put another man in the hospital for repairs, but not the nuncio. I felt Erit clinging partially to me and partially to the back of the drone. We started abruptly to move, and it was, I admit, a terrifying way to travel. Drones are space vehicles, not meant to carry passengers. This was one of our largest, four meters long by one in diameter, and the only handholds were the coolant wings and the laser-beam drill. It was a device meant to supply tools and power for external repairs on Ariane's hull in space. As an air car, it was bad news.

At one hundred meters high, a terrifying altitude to anyone so insecurely fastened to a flying machine as we were, the drone bolted suddenly south and seaward, toward our rendezvous with Ariane off Zodiac Bay. I saw the city lights whirl and blur beneath us. Then we were almost dislodged by the sudden acceleration and the rush of night wind, and the university acropolis simply vanished in the mist of the low overcast rolling in from the sea.

I could feel Erit doing the Vulkish muscle disciplines that deaden fatigue and fear, and I felt the alien girl's fingers digging into my shoulder. My silly student's wig went flying off into the night. The frigid ocean air blasted my naked thighs under my kilt. I was terrified and miserable and at the same time exhilarated and intoxicated with my own heroics. I had a fleeting thought about the horror with which Lady Nora would regard the night's activities, and then I put the thought out of my mind and promised myself not to worry again about what my mother would think—not until all this was over.

I locked my legs around the drone, for all the world like some absurd parody of one of my warman ancestors gripping his battle mare. We couldn't have been traveling very fast or we would have been blown off and directly down some half a kilometer into the Gonlan Sea. But it felt as though we were making kilolights through the night and cloud. And then we climbed out of the stratus undercast into clear air, and I could see the glow of the galactic lens and the distant, distant fuzzy brightness of the Magellanic Clouds, and it was so beautiful that I forgot to be frightened. I simply held on to the half-naked girl in my arms and shouted with delight.

Erit's Vulkish cloak whipped in the wind across my shoulders, and I felt the alien's face close to mine. I looked through the darkness and saw the gleam of silver. Her eyes were open, and she was looking at me, no longer afraid, but simply beautiful. We climbed higher and higher, as in a wonderful and nerve-scraping dream of night flight, and the air grew bitterly cold and I could feel the girl's slender body shivering, but there was nothing I could do to warm her. It was all I could do to hold us all on the curving back of the drone.

And then I heard the sonic boom of Ariane's reentry and saw the glowing ionization trail she left across the sky as she came down to us. And in that blue light I saw, also, that the alien girl was smiling. Her fear was gone, and her teeth showed whitely in the darkness. *Lord Star*, I thought, *what* human *woman could make so swift a transition from bewildered terror to strength? Where, in all the universe, were people like this one made?*

"That, Starkahn," Ariane said against my skull, "is exactly what we intend to find out." She had been spying on me all the way from Gonlanburg.

Chapter Nine

The time of the black starship, or the Year of the Death, as it came to be called, was not only a time of peril, but one of deep social change. Those transitions taking place within the fiber of society were not readily apparent to contemporaries; to an historian *they would have been obvious.*

> Vikus-Bel Cyb 1009, *The Symbiotic Culture*,
> early Confederate period

A time will come, brethren, when even the Empire and the Order will have outlived their usefulness. This is not treason, but prophecy.

> St. Emeric of Rhada, *The Dialogues*,
> early Second Stellar Empire period

We orbited Rhada at a mean distance of 11,000 kilometers, out of range of all but the most deliberate search. I sat on the ill-fitting contour in Ariane's bridge and listened to the exchange of messages among the various minor units of the Fleet in Rhadan space.

It was inevitable, of course, that our original flight plan, the one we had filed on Gonlan to the Omicron satellite and then to the Rhada sun had come under some very close scrutiny by the Fleet authorities when Ariane failed to arrive on time. Now, judging by the radio traffic, the planetary controllers were beginning to suspect that something was amiss. Either someone had filed a false flight plan or a small starship was missing. A slow but gradually increasing shock was traveling through the axons and dendrites of the intrastellar navigational network. Soon, if the trauma were not corrected (by someone finding the missing vessel), the tremor would jump the provincial boundaries and reach Fleet Sector headquarters, and from there it would flash swiftly to Command, where some note was taken of all Imperial units in this spiral of the galaxy. And finally, it would jar the powers that be in Nyor, at Grand Fleet headquarters on Earth.

All of this would be vastly hastened when the sluggish Gonlan controllers realized that the ship that filed the original plan had been none other than Cyb-ADSPS 339, partner and companion to the Starkahn of Rhada.

I was genuinely sorry for the trouble we were causing: trouble that would get far worse before it got better. But I had spent a lifetime heeding the warnings and accepting the advice of Rhada's Royal Vulk. Fleet discipline was strong in me (well, reasonably so for a Rim noble), but my belief in Gret was absolute. The Vulk, with his perspective of millennia, was more to be believed than a fanatical Navigator, an expedient Galacton, or an ambitious mother. (*Forgive me, Lady Nora,* I thought. *But it is true.*)

"What's happening on the ground?" I asked Ariane. "Can't you extend the sensors?"

"Not without risking detection," she replied. "It is best to let Erit handle it."

"Yes," I told myself, "Erit could reach Gret through the mind-touch." But Gret was old and sick, immobile in his tank of gel. What could we expect if the Vulks' mind-link failed?

I stared distractedly through the transparent walls of the bridge. The nebulosity of the galactic lens was very distinct—it was difficult to think of it as what it really was: a swirl of a billion stars, some few million with planets, some few thousand of those populated by men. Yet even with that winnowing, the number of my kind in the galaxy was staggering. And each one, each life, stood in mortal danger from the apparently random attacks of the black starship.

I looked away from the lens and back to Rhada: a blue world of seas and some green and brown lands. White cloud patterns, brilliant against the sun-gleaming oceans, mottled the surface. From this distance the works of man were invisible. The planet hung in interstellar space, silent, seemingly without motion, a great blue-green gem flecked with the colors of soil and sand and mountain. It was said Earth herself once looked like that before the city of Nyor grew to cover almost the entire surface of the world.

Yet the black starship could infect the Rhada sun with some stellar death, and within hours Rhada's clouds and seas would boil off into the void and the land would first parch and then melt and finally vaporize as the clouds of white-hot plasma, the hot guts of the sun, laved over it with the speed of light.

When one thought on it, the science involved was massive—but not superhuman. The warlocks of my own time knew how to kill stars—in theory. It was simply that we had never, even in our Dark Time, considered undertaking murder on so vast a scale. Questions filled my mind, questions only a Triad of Gret-Erit and the silver-eyed girl could answer. Where was the black starship now? Where had it

come from? How much longer could it function? And over
and over again—*why?* Why had such an engine of destruction been built?

I turned impatiently to the bridge valve, half expecting
to see Erit. But the Vulk had taken the girl into such seclusion as Ariane's interior offered the moment we'd come
aboard.

I scratched irritably at the interfaces between my own
flesh and the gill tubes that still protruded from my chest.
There had been no possibility of finding a technician to
remove the waterlung implanted in my chest. I could feel
the slight chill of the cryogenic carbon dioxide scrubber
against the inside of my rib wall. I was struck by the matter-
of-fact way we accepted the great changes life had brought
in the last few centuries. The artificial gill in my chest was
a case in point—a minor one, but it was part of a technology
and a *Zeitgeist* that might, in time, bring down the Empire
itself and all other familiar human social forms. A thousand
years earlier, my ancestors would have been shocked and
horrified at the thought of undergoing casual surgery for
such things as implanting the means to breath water—simply for sport. Those same ancestors would regard Ariane
as some sort of horrible hybrid creature, part robot, part
monster. In fact, my namesake, Kier the Rebel, became a
racial hero by killing a cyborg in ritual combat during Marlana's rebellion. And the alien girl—how easily we accepted
the obvious fact that she was only conditionally human, that
she was some sort of mutant, but still a living, thinking
(and very beautiful) fellow creature with whom we must
communicate and learn to cooperate, lest her black starship
kill us all. Even in Kynan the Navigator's time, the instinc-
tive response would have been one of hatred, fear, and
retributive murder.

Of course, I thought, not all humans were so willing to
meet this challenge peaceably. I remembered the stony fanaticism of Nav Peter and thought of the political pusillan-
imity of Sokolovsky Bel-Ami, our great (and short-sighted)
Galacton.

*   *   *

Ariane, with half of her systems lying idle as we orbited the planet, was in a ruminative mood. Perhaps it was our situation, or perhaps it was the fact that the silver-eyed alien was aboard, but she spoke to me in her most feminine and seductive voice: a veritable whisper from the console speakers.

"Do you realize, Kier, that it was hardly more than two months ago that we were surveying Delphinus? It seems much, much longer than that."

Since a cyborg has one of the most keenly developed senses of time passage imaginable, I could only assume that Ariane was speaking figuratively—and reply in the same mood. "We were having an argument about Nav Anselm Styr, weren't we?"

"Not really an argument. We don't argue, Kier."

I considered that statement for a while before risking a reply. "Well," I said finally, "sometimes we have discussions."

"No more than that," the cyborg said dreamily.

"Are you all right, Ariane?" I asked worriedly.

"Of course."

I blanked out the walls and played with a holograph of near space. We didn't dare use our instruments, and for Erit to contact Gret comfortably, we had to wait for the planet below to rotate under us. The lands of the Rhad family were still beyond the sunlit limb of the watery world we orbited. Ariane said, "You seem nervous, Kier."

"I can't imagine why I should be," I said with a touch of sarcasm. "We are deserters from the Fleet, kidnapers, priest-attackers, hospital robbers, and the Star knows what else we are being accused of at this moment. Why should I be the slightest bit nervous?"

"That isn't the reason," the cyborg said evenly.

"Meaning what?"

"The girl. She's what makes you jittery." There was an edge of resentment in Ariane's voice.

"You can't mean it," I said.

"She's very beautiful, of course. In a *human* way." By all the little stars and comets, there was a touch of archness in Ariane's manner. A dash of—jealousy. Yes, my cyborg partner was jealous of the alien.

"My interest is purely practical," I said. Then I wondered why I said something so obviously as untrue as that. Ariane, of all persons, would know me well enough to know what I was feeling—even before I, myself, might put it into perspective.

"You should have seen yourself when you came aboard," Ariane said. "Like a cadet on his first rendezvous."

"That was one hellishly exciting ride you gave us on the drone, Cyb Ari," I said, using her formal title for the first time in weeks.

"It was the girl," Ariane said stubbornly. Then she added darkly, "If this were back in the olden days you like so well, she would probably be burned as witch. Just because of those silver eyes."

"She's obviously a mutant," I said stiffly. It wasn't like Ariane to carry on like this. "You've seen human mutations before."

"None like that one," Ariane said. "You know," she went on obliquely, "I could look like that if I chose."

That was approximately true, of course. An ADSPS cyborg, after his or her tour of duty, could ask to be reintegrated into a humanoid form and programmed to lead a planetary life. Not many did, but it *was* possible.

"You mean you'd trade the freedom you have—*our* freedom to roam the whole galaxy—just for a pretty girl's figure?" I was so aghast at the thought that I lost track of the fact that the only reintegration and reprogramming we could look forward to now was the criminal code variety.

Ariane didn't, however, and she began to laugh. It was familiar, warm laughter, far more human than cyborg, and it relieved me because it indicated that her mood was passing and she was acting more like herself and less like an imitation of a jealous wife.

She made a humming sound that indicated derision, and

she said,"Well, we mustn't quarrel before our guests, Starkahn. Erit has finished with our victim, and they are about
to join us. I hope you can withstand the shock at such close
range. But I forget—you brought her aboard clutched to
your bosom, didn't you?"

Before I could make adequate reply to that, the bridge
valve dilated, and Erit came through, leading the alien. A
suit of Fleet-issue work coveralls had never looked better
than on that small but ample form.

Erit's featureless face was deeply lined. She was obviously fatigued from her long session with the alien girl
and with who could tell what other personal concerns. One
tended, in dealing with the Vulks, to forget their deep in-
terdependence and the paucity of their numbers throughout
the galaxy. Gret's debility was a source of concern to me—
and to every Rhadan, for the ancient creature was inextric-
ably involved with our history as a nation and a people. But
to another Vulk, most particularly to Erit, who had shared
the very essence of his being in a way no human could ever
completely understand, his weakness threatened a loss of
self. Yet, in the manner of her race, Erit was devoting herself
almost completely to our human problems.

Erit, slender, sexless, familiar in tunic and kilt, made
the formal gesture of recognition and spoke quietly. "Starkahn, I bring you Marissa Tran Wyeth, Watcher of the Third
Death." The name was strange with its exotic Anglic clicks
and sibilants, and the patronymic "Tran" was unknown to
me. There were none among the star families so named.
But the title "Watcher of the Third Death" shook me. It had
a threatening sound to one who had actually seen the black
starship in action.

The girl made a peculiar twisting obeisance, a rigid gesture that was more wary maneuver than respectful salute to
my rank. She regarded me evenly with those marvelous
silver eyes. "The strange creature you call a Vulk has told
me many marvels," she said in a low, musical voice. "Perhaps they are true, perhaps not. If you are truly a king, you
will not lie to me." Her hypno-learned *lingua spacia* was

heavily accented with Anglic, but not with modern Anglic. Rather she spoke with the accents heard now only in the recordings of voices of the First Empire.

"The Vulk don't lie," I said. "Whatever Erit has taught you is the truth." I was filled with questions, anxious to pump the girl's brain dry of facts. The Star knew how badly we needed them, with her deadly machine loose among the inhabited worlds. But Erit's mind brushed mine softly with a note of caution, and I remembered that no matter how strange the silver-eyed mutant seemed to us, we must seem infinitely stranger to her. I would have to go carefully with her.

"This is a small vessel," the girl said, walking slowly about Ariane's bridge. There was a touch of scorn in her tone as she inspected the unfamiliar instruments in the tiny control room. "Is it a warship?"

"Yes. Of a sort."

"Imperial." Her lip curled with deep hatred.

"A unit of the Fleet," I said neutrally, wondering what she remembered of her awakening in the laboratories of the Gonlani warlocks and our wild flight on the drone.

She stood before me and studied my eyes. "Are you *all* Genies, then? All blue-eyed supermen?" There was a universe of racial anger in her voice.

I looked helplessly at Erit. The Vulk said quietly, "Eugenicists."

For a moment I didn't understand what she was saying. Then my years of grubbing through remote historical events came to my rescue. Long ago, so long ago no one knew exactly when, a party of eugenic fanatics had dominated the government of the First Empire. But they were legendary, as were so many things that happened before the Dark Time, that uncounted number of years or centuries or even millennia that separated the Second Stellar Empire from the First. I searched my memory for more details and found them. They were part fact, part rumor and legend. In the expanding days of the First Stellar Empire the Eugenicists— the *Genies,* as they were popularly called—prevailed on

the galactic government to "improve the race" by trans-
porting criminals, dissenters, and (I had no doubt) political
opponents out of the main galaxy. For five hundred years
these unfortunates took "the Long Death"—the trip to the
Lesser Magellanic Cloud. But since the voyage took three
hundred years even at light speeds, no word of a safe arrival
in the Cloud had ever reached the main galaxy. Then, in
the political upheavals of the time, something called "the
Concerned Coalition" had stopped the transports. But nothing more was ever heard of the transportees, and, in time,
they were all but forgotten.

"You know and the eyeless one knows what I mean,"
the girl said coldly. "But why have you suffered *her* to live?
She is small, deformed, obviously a mutation—not human,
not *perfect*."

"Erit is a Vulk," I said, controlling my anger. Among
the Rhad no one spoke so of the Vulk.

"A word," the girl said, her face shut and hostile.

Was it possible that this person knew nothing of the Vulk?
It hardly seemed credible. The Vulk had been among men
since before the Interregnum.

"She knows nothing about us, Starkahn," Erit said.

"But what *does* she know?" I asked in Rhadan.

"Her mind is well guarded. It needs Triad to delve into
it deeply."

Marissa listened to our exchange, in a language she obviously did not understand, with deep suspicion. I couldn't
let that emotion deepen and build an impenetrable wall
between us. I needed too desperately to know what she
could tell me.

I said, "There have been no Eugenicists among men
for—" I was almost at a loss to guess at how long it had
been. Nearly ten thousand years, certainly, for the Vulk had
been among us for at least that long. I tried to recall that
obscure period of human history—it could have been no
more than five hundred years in duration—when the Eugenicist party dominated the First Empire. Lord Star, it
would take some deep searching among my books and

tapes—none of which were aboard Ariane now—to discover the source of this girl's hatred for us. I finished lamely,
"There have been none for many lifetimes. Everything is
changed."

"Who rules in Nyor?" the girl asked suddenly. Perhaps
she was beginning to understand how long she had lain in
that support capsule. It would be a terrible shock to her
when the realization was complete. I glanced apprehensively
at Erit, but the Vulk only shrugged as if to say that the girl
must learn at her own pace.

"Sokolovsky Bel-Ami is Galacton," I said.

The name obviously meant nothing to her. "The Raschilds are gone? After all they did to destroy millions, they
simply died like common folk?" There was a world of satisfaction and grim pleasure in her question. It shook me
badly. The last of the Raschild Galactons died after the
Second Aliya, the second great wave of stellar colonization
when the First Empire was still young. It gave me some
historical perspective on Marissa Tran Wyeth's temporal
frame, and the knowledge was shocking. She was speaking
of a time in human history so remote that only scholars
specializing in exotica even knew of it.

"Marissa," I said as gently as I knew how. "The last
Raschild died a hundred centuries ago."

The girl sat down on the edge of the control couch abruptly,
as though I had cut her legs from under her. The silver eyes
went dark, and her pale lips parted. "You are lying to me,"
she whispered. "You are lying, Genie—"

"He speaks the truth," Erit said. "It is as I suspected.
You were meant to sleep in your capsule only a short time.
It was three hundred ES years. Isn't that so?"

Marissa's breath was sharply indrawn, and I knew that
Erit's question had struck home. It all fell neatly into place
for me, and I wondered why it was that I had not thought
of it before. The reason was obvious, of course: the time
span involved clogged the imagination. But as a spaceman
and a student of history, I should have had enough flexibility
of mind to realize that time had no meaning on the cosmic

scale. In a universe where light took five hundred centuries to travel from the end of one arm of the galaxy to another, what mattered a mere ten thousand years? What were "years" anyway? An arbitrary measurement of time at best, a unit taken by men from the astronomy of their home planet (a small planet of an obscure star, at that) to slice up the illimitable and immortal cosmos. In such a moment of insight, one caught some glimmer of man's unbelievable arrogance. In this, the Navigators were right. The universe alone was holy, and, in a very real sense, the means to understand it and to voyage through its grandeur, the telescopes and starships, were sacred.

But no moment of soaring realization could, for me, lessen the human shock of realizing that this frail girl was from the *Magellanic Cloud*.

Chapter Ten

*We are the discarded ones, the generations of the lost.
The plasma storms between the galaxies invaded our
parents and changed our structure, but not our
hearts—which are filled with anger. Ours is the rage
of the segregated and the abandoned, and it is righ-
teous rage, my children. In this place we will build
such an empire as no man has ever seen before. On
these bleak rocks we will build a nation. And in that
nation we will build death for the oppressors.*
> Marius Tran Rosse, Arriver,
> Captain of the Communes of Magellan,
> 6345 A.D.-6420 A.D.,
> early First Empire period

*—to this date we have dispatched no fewer than three
thousand four hundred starships past the Rim, a mil-*

*lion five hundred thousand souls into limbo. And what
has been the result? Has this enormous expenditure
lessened crime or dissent? Has this gigantic effort
brought tranquility to the Empire? It has not. Eco-
nomically, Transportation has been a disaster. Mor-
ally, it is genocide.* It must end!

> Golden Age fragment found at Tel-Califia, Earth.
> Believed to be part of a manifesto of the
> Concerned Coalition, early First Empire period

"The world you thought you were returning to has been
dead and fragmented ten thousand years, Marissa," the Vulk
said wearily. "There are no Raschilds, no Genies, no transports. All that died long long ago." I watched the girl with
admiration for her steadiness. How many of the nobles and
great ones I knew could take such a pronouncement with
her courage? She stood against a console, unmoving, her
silvery eyes dark and filled with a grief that I could only
dimly understand.

To know that you had arrived at the end of a long
journey—a journey from which there could be no return—
was one thing. But to know that this same journey had thrust
you a hundred thousand lifetimes forward in time, isolated
you utterly—that was a blow beyond human bearing.

But, I realized suddenly, she *wasn't* human—not completely. Somewhere in the intergalactic abyss, the germ plasm
of her ancestors had been changed into—what? *Homo Magellansis.*

"The communes," she said in a hushed voice. "What of
the communes of Magellan?"

"We know nothing of any such communes, Marissa," I
said gently. "Most of our people have never heard even of
Transportation. The practice ended five hundred years after
it began."

I could see her struggling with the confusing time values
involved now. She said, "My great grandparents were First
Arrivers. They took the Long Death in 6350."

For a moment I didn't understand what she meant, and

then I translated her archaic dating system into my own and the shock deepened. "Six thousand Anno Domini—we don't use that form any longer, Marissa—but six thousand A.D. was the first year of the Galactic Era. This is 8760 G.E."

The girl closed her eyes and touched her throat in a softly human gesture. Her early anger was lost now, drowned in a sea of terrible enlightenment. *"So long?"* she murmured.

"Longer, even, than that," Erit said. "For between the First Empire and our own came the Interregnum, the Dark Time, and no one, not even my people, know how long that black age lasted."

Her sorrow and loneliness struck me. It was like a wave of cobalt sadness. I don't know how else to express it. It had *color* and a grieving *feel* to it. I realize I express it badly, but it is because for a human being there are no words to describe sadness. Every man and woman alive in the galaxy can suffer grief, but who can transmit it to another? Words simply won't do. Yet the girl projected her emotion to me, and I felt it almost as she did. Much more than eyes the color of silver separated us in *kind.* Yet her mutation made it possible—no, *imperative*—that I share what she was feeling.

And though I cannot take credit for realizing it then, the experience later gave me some insight into how it was possible for a whole people, all the children of those who had "died the Long Death," to live in communes with *one* heart and mind, with *one* aspiration. Here and now it was sadness, grief, a young girl's loneliness. But *there* and *then* it was revenge and hatred for the uncaring society that had rejected them. That was the function of the Magellanic Mutation: to share and project one's emotions. In such a society there could be no conflict of purpose. And such a society could, and *did,* build not one but *three* of the great black starships. Marissa described her worlds.

"They are—were? How can I know?—bleak lands, but rich in metals and minerals. My home was on the Fifth Commune, the fourth planet of a double star. We lived together, always together, all of us. We were one. We were a *family,* a family of millions. We hated the people of the main galaxy, but we loved one another—" And as she said it and felt it, *I* felt it, too: that sense of belonging, of community. It was a strange and terrible experience, though there was more to come later. But even then I felt the strangeness of a deep love for my fellow beings and a rabid hatred of those "outside," the callous and materialistic billions of the main galaxy who had cast "us" out.

As we rested in the control pod of Ariane, orbiting my home world, I had that strange feeling that I was living two lives—my own and Marissa's. I had shared my mind before, with the Vulk. But this was a different experience. It was emotion I shared and, in a way, therefore, greater understanding than I had ever shared before with another being.

Yet I retained my own identity and my own critical faculty. And it was this that bared the obvious, tragic flaw in the world of communes she described to us in such glowing, grieving words.

They had been cast out of the main galaxy for dissent. The powers called it criminality, but, truthfully, it was a matter of definition. And perhaps the galactic universal Spirit, whatever one recognizes as God, or Prime Mover, or what-have-you, intervened. As their fathers and mothers took the Long Death, their genes were changed and the Magellanic Mutation was born. I'm a soldier and an historian, not a mystic. But who can say what is chance and what is teleology? Dissent caused their expulsion. The mutation made dissent unbearable. Whatever they *felt,* they projected to one another, and so a mass consciousness was born. In our race's dimmest history, there have been political systems that attempted to *force* communism or community on men. They all failed because man in the main galaxy was never anything but man: vital, quarrelsome, avaricious, predatory (ask the Vulk about that!), and *individualistic.* The people of the Cloud, *Homo Magellansis,* could not live that way. The mutation made it impossible.

"Life in the communes was aways hard," Marissa said, and I felt her terrible longing to see the double sun and share herself with her fellows, "but we were *together*. We worked together, ate and made love together, learned together—"

"And hated together," I said. Her silver eyes flashed for a moment, and I felt her anger, too. Even Erit shivered.

"Yes, that, too. We needed that to build the *Deaths*."

"Your starship," I said cautiously.

She nodded. "It was the greatest honor to be chosen a Watcher. To go with one of the *Deaths*."

My mouth felt dry as I asked her, "How many were built, Marissa?"

"Mine was the third. You know nothing of the first two?"

"Nothing. We found you in Delphinus. The ship—the *Death*—had been damaged slightly. Perhaps that was why the machines never woke you."

She sagged. "Then the others crashed. Or never reached the main galaxy."

"No such great starships were ever discovered in the galaxy before," I said. "Not until we found yours."

"So it was all for nothing," she said bitterly. "Each generation slaved to build a *Death* that the next generation might launch. But even in my time, the desire for revenge was weakening. The work on *Death Four* was far, far behind schedule when I entered the capsule."

It was strange and terrible to hear her speak of things that happened so far, far off in space and time as though they had taken place yesterday and nearby.

And I gave thought to the cosmic irony, the tragedy really, of an entire civilization dedicated to building nothing for themselves but the mightiest engines of destruction the mind could conceive—for revenge on a world that barely outlasted their First Arrivers, had they but known it. It was a fit subject for cosmic, universal, and bitter, bitter laughter.

The silver eyes searched for mine and held them, and I felt a gentle pity for what I saw there. "The Genies," she said, "the Raschilids. All of that. Dust for a hundred centuries?"

"Yes," I replied.

"While I slept in the capsule—"

"Yes," I said again, not knowing how to comfort such sadness.

"And my people never returned."

"Never."

"Perhaps," Erit said quietly, "they lost the need for vengeance. Perhaps they turned inward, into the Cloud. There is a whole galaxy out there to know, to live in. A billion stars. Perhaps they did that."

The girl began to weep silently. Her tears were tinged with the same silvery color as her eyes. They were like drops of molten starlight on her cheeks. I thought she was the most beautiful thing, and the saddest, that I have ever known. I touched her cheek more gently, more tenderly, than I have ever touched a human being of my own kind.

"This is enlightening, I'm sure." Ariane's voice came into the control pod tinged with some impatience. "But the business at hand is that ship."

The Magellanic girl jerked with sudden fright. Her eyes went wide. "Who spoke?"

"Ariane," I said. "The ship."

"The *ship?*" Marissa looked about the bridge in utter confusion.

"Ariane Cyb-ADSPS 339," I said, not realizing how my matter-of-fact statement might startle one knowing nothing of starship cyborgs.

"Your vessel is *alive?*" Marissa's expression showed clearly she thought such a thing impossible, almost unthinkable.

"Surely you know of cyborgs," I said. "There were humanoid cyborgs—" I almost said "in your time" but curbed myself.

She looked about her at the curving bulkheads of the pod. Erit permitted herself a weary smile.

"A living starship," the girl said almost to herself, filled with a sense of wonder.

"For our work it is the only possible arrangement," I said. "We spend months—sometimes years—alone in deep space. One needs—a companion. *You* should understand that."

"A robot?" Her fright had passed swiftly, and her scientific curiosity was aroused. I thought that marvelous.

"Not a robot," Ariane said crisply. "A cyborg. Quite a different thing. A cyborg *and* a citizen."

"It is a time of wonders," the Magellanic girl said in her archaically accented *lingua spacia*.

"It is a time of great danger," Erit said. "And the danger is from your vessel."

"Where is my ship?" the girl asked suddenly. "What has been done with the *Death?*"

"Nothing has been done with it," I said, with sinking heart. "And we hoped that you would know where it is and how it can be stopped. That is why we took you from the warlocks on Gonlanburg. That, too, is why the Navigators want you. Is it possible you don't know what the *Death's* mission was?"

The girl's face darkened. "The mission was to kill."

"That, I know. I saw what your weapons did to the Delphinus sun."

"The *Death* is functioning?"

"Too well. It attacked Sigma Libra. There was a Fleet outpost on an outermost Sigma planet. It is vapor now." Now it was her turn to feel my emotions, and they were laced with anger, bitterness, and frustration. I had been so certain that the girl would be the key to unlock the mystery of the murderous starship, and now I was unsure.

It evidently puzzled her and took a moment for her to understand we meant nothing occult when we used the word "warlock." I explained. "Scientists. Since the Interregnum we have been speaking of them so. They were sometimes burned for researching. Gonlanburg is a province of my nation, Rhada. It was from the university there we took you. They were going to turn you over to the clergy."

"Are you still savages, then?"

"Somewhat," I said drily. "Most particularly when there is a doomsday machine loose in the galaxy."

Marissa turned to Erit. "You are—a Vulk?"

"I am," Erit said.

"You are different. Yet you've been allowed to live? Among men?"

"We have had troubles. But that was long ago. We live without fear now."

Damn, I thought. Was the girl actually testing human tolerance? Here and now? But what better time, I considered. A human being, a Vulk, and a cyborg—working and living as one. And now, hopefully—desperately—a Magellanic?

"The teachings of a lifetime are not easily put aside," the girl said. "And I am a Watcher. My indoctrination was very firm."

"I don't doubt it," I said. "But your enemies are dead. And your ship is killing *my* people. It must be stopped."

The girl regarded me curiously. "Are you perhaps a cyborg, too?"

She was looking at the blunt ends of the stoppered gill implanted in my chest.

"No," I said impatiently. "It is an implant. I was on a water world, and the implant allows me to breathe water— that is all. It will come out when I have time to have it removed."

Marissa shook her head wonderingly and said, "'O brave new world that has such people in 't!'"

Lord Star, Ruler of the Universe! I thought. *We stand on the brink of annihilation and the girl quotes Dawn Age poets to me.* But it was a remarkable and wonderful thing to do, really. I was certain I had never met anyone with such equanimity and courage. Yes, she was *brave.* Maybe one became that way by sharing himself or herself with his or her fellow beings. It was something to think about—even here and now.

"Lady Tran Wyeth—" I began formally, but she interrupted me with the first real smile I had seen from her: a lovely sight, too. "There were no Imperial titles and townsman's speech where I came from. There is no need for them here. My name is Marissa."

"Marissa, then." I began again and told her all that I thought she might not know of what had happened since Ariane and I discovered her and her grimly named vessel in Delphinus. When I had done, I said, "There is nothing in the Grand Fleet that can stand against your ship if it is programmed to fight—"

"It is," she interrupted quietly. "The function of a Watcher was only to start the battle computers after the intergalactic flight. And to see that all else is in order."

"And then?"

Her eyes lightened momentarily with that communal fervor. "Why then, the Watcher dies. We have a Cause."

"You *had* a Cause," I said heavily. "What you have now is a duty."

"A duty? To what? I did not ask to be brought here."

"You have a duty to the people who will die if you do not stop your vessel—people who have done you and yours no harm. These are a generation thousands of years unborn when you left the Cloud."

She lowered her head and rested in silence, once more alone, a creature far out of her time and place.

Presently she said, "Have you star charts?"

"Ariane," I said. Instantly, the pod darkened, and Ariane projected a holograph of Delphinian space before us. Once again, the Magellanic girl stared in surprise.

"It *is* the Dolphin," she said in a hushed tone, looking at the constellation in miniature.

"A projection from the region of the constellation of Sagittarius—where Earth is located," I said. "Do you want to see it from another angle?"

The girl shook her head slowly. "It would do no good— What did the small creature call you? I have forgotten your name—" She sounded suddenly very tired, and I realized she was still not strong after her long sleep in the capsule. We would have to treat her gently.

"I am called Kier Veg-Rhad," I said.

"Kier." She spoke the name curiously. "Kier, I cannot read these stars. Have you no maps?"

"We don't use maps," I said. "Ariane could make some, I suppose. But it would take some time."

We seemed to have reached an absurd impasse. The vast gulf between her technology and ours separated us. She wanted what were, to Ariane and me, fantastically outmoded aids to stellar navigation.

"There is no time," she said. "The *Death* has begun its program if it struck the Dolphin star. But the next—you called it 'Sigma Libra'? It should have been the Craddock Sun—"

My odd store of historical oddities came to my rescue again. "Sigma Libra was once called Craddock—it was named by a First Empire survey man."

"There was a Genie colony there when my great-grandparents took the Long Death," Marissa said. "The *Death* was programmed to strike it down."

"What colonies there were in Sigma Libra were abandoned generations ago when the ice covered the only inner planet rich enough to warrant exploitation. All that was left was the Fleet station on the outermost world." I couldn't help adding, "There were brave men and women there, doing a lonely job. Your vessel killed them."

"We will achieve nothing by stirring up new enmities, Starkahn," Erit murmured.

Marissa, however, did a strange thing. She touched my hand in what seemed some sort of ritual gesture and said, "For the death of your comrades, my death, if you will it."

"I don't want your death, girl," I said exasperatedly. "I want your help, and quickly."

"It is our way of making amends," she said softly.

I couldn't help asking, "And did they often take up the option, your communal brothers and sisters?"

She shook her head slowly. "Never. Only the state had the right to kill—for the good of the commune."

What glimpses of a strange, disciplined, frightening—and yet stirring—world she gave me. A people in love with death.

"Kier," Ariane said. "If she can give me the attack program and we can translate the old names of the stars, we can find the starship."

"If we find it, Marissa," I asked, "can we stop it?"

"I can."

"You? *Only* you?"

"The ship will accept only a Watcher. When the capsule is broken, the program is complete."

"Ariane," I said in a fever of anxiety. "Get the names. And, Erit—the planet below has turned. Will you want a commo assist to reach Gret?"

I had turned away from Erit for a moment only, but when I looked back, my heart sank, for the small Vulk had sunk to the deck of the pod in rigid silence in the position of mourning.

Only once before had I ever seen a Vulk in that formalized position: knees bent and together, body contracted with supple grief, head hidden in folded arms. In Triad with Gret-Erit, I had crossed time and space to a world that no longer existed, Vulka. And there, through the minds and memories of my tri-symbiotes, I had witnessed the death rituals of the Vulkish people. In that posture alone did the Vulk mourn their dead. Once they had kneeled so in thousands as the humans butchered them in the great Vulk pogroms of the Interregnum.

Now it could mean only one thing, and the sense of loss that washed over me was almost too much to bear. Five thousand years of Rhadan history rested there on Ariane's deck, five thousand years of the history of my family and their world and all the worlds they helped to win and hold for the Galactons of Nyor. That, and much more, for the Vulk were virtually immortal. Virtually, but not quite. The world below us had turned, and Erit's mind had reached out eagerly to her brother-husband—to find only emptiness.

That was why Erit mourned. Below, in a chamber in a house by a pounding sea, memories of Kier the Rebel and Kynan the Navigator had ceased. Gret, the Royal Vulk of Rhada, was dead.

Chapter Eleven

Some life of men unblest
He knew, which made him droop, and fill'd his head.
He went; his piping took a troubled sound
Of storms that rage outside our happy ground;
He could not wait their passing, he is dead.
> Matthew Arnold, *Thyrsis*, Dawn Age poet,
> from a printed book discovered near
> Biblios Brittanis, Mars,
> early Confederate period

Of this be sure, my friend and wife, brother-sister,
son and father: Where you are, there will I be also.
For I cannot die while you remember me. So say the
mists, and the sea, and the golden, golden suns of
Home.

Vulk lament, authorship unknown,
period unknown

*Men found a single being among all the stars, and he
persecuted him, and killed him in thousands, and used
him. And Vulk called Man:* Friend.
  St. Emeric of Rhada, Grand Master of Navigators,
  early Second Stellar Empire period

For a moment all was forgotten in our grief. I shared Erit's
loss, and the girl from the Cloud shared mine—the Magellanic Mutation did not spare her—and Ariane, too, remembered Gret.

Below us, I knew, all of Rhada was deep in mourning,
and I wanted desperately to leave orbit and go down to my
family and my people. I could almost hear the funeral drums
and see the buildings draped in somber white, for that is
how we Rhadans honor our history, and the ancient Vulk
who died that day was certainly part of our past. He had
been the first star king's fool, and the second king's friend,
and the friend and servant and teacher of all the Rhadan
kings who came after.

But we dared not go down, not even to take Erit to the
side of the sepulcher, not even for that. Instead, I threw
caution aside and used the communicator. If I could not
honor my teacher, at least I could risk that much.

My mother's tear-stained face appeared in the holograph,
and that gave some indication of the spasm of sadness that
was wracking our homeland. I had never before seen the
Lady Nora Veg-Rhad shed tears, never.

She said sadly, "The nation is in mourning. And where
are you, Starkahn? Your place is here."

"I cannot come," I said regretfully.

My mother's patrician face turned hard beneath her grief.
"You dishonor your friend, Kier," she said bitterly.

"Gret would understand the need," I said, wanting, really,
to tell her that I was still, in a sense, acting under the Vulk's
instructions.

"Gret is dead, Starkahn," Lady Nora said. "After five thousand years in the service of the Rhad, he is dead and in his bier. And you *cannot* abandon some wild, unsanctioned scheme to pay him respect?"

To call what we were about "unsanctioned" was a typically Noraesque flight into what I sometimes, in my more rebellious moments, called "parentally controlled reality." I was engaged in something not only unsanctioned but also dangerous, illegal, and quite possibly impossible. I was at odds with the authorities on Gonlan, with my superiors in the Fleet, with the council of Rhada, with the Order of Navigators, and, apparently, with my mother. But she, noblewoman of the Empire, could not admit that her son was a fugitive and kidnaper, and, to some, a deserter. My actions, therefore, were "unsanctioned." Come home, do the expected thing, be conventional—and (with Lady Nora's influence at work) all will be forgiven the Starkahn of Rhada.

Except that the Starkahn and give or take a few billion other people would very likely be dead within the year, incinerated by an exploded sun.

"I cannot come down to Rhada, Lady," I said again. "Not yet."

Lady Nora seemed genuinely distressed. Her holograph shivered slightly as she impatiently worked the sensors of her unit to clear my image. "Where are you, Kier?" she demanded.

I shook my head. "Within commo range. That is all I can tell you."

I could see the sudden flush of anger mingling with her already aroused emotions. The Lady Nora Veg-Rhad—who in other times would have been Queen of Rhada—did not like to be balked, and most particularly not by her son.

"The authorities are very angry, Kier," she said. "I can't blame them or even stop them from taking action if you do not return to Rhada at once."

"I'm sorry, Mother," I said.

Lady Nora's expression changed, grew haughty and

scornful, and she said, in a voice that used to terrify me when I was a child and still sometimes brought tremors of self-doubt, "Ah, then. You, in your wisdom, in your *mature judgment,* have concluded that your superior officers in the Fleet, the learned warlocks of Gonlanburg University, the local Imperial administration, *and* the Order of Navigators are all wrong and you are right. Only *you* know what is to be done about that *thing* you discovered in space. I can't believe my ears."

I swallowed hard and said, "I'm not the only one, Lady Nora."

"Naturally, I had forgotten your cyborg." It wasn't often that Lady Nora's deeply buried thread of anticybism surfaced. And in fairness, she regarded Ariane highly, even felt some affection for her, and was, under certain circumstances, willing to commit me to the cyborg's care. Yet when she grew really angry or when she was frustrated and prevented from obtaining the instant compliance with her commands she thought was her due, she became very like other human women when confronted with "those SW pilots and their cyborgs." Perhaps, I thought, given the nature of human beings, it was natural to think a close human-cyborg affinity *un*natural.

"Ariane," I said quietly. "You'll forgive my mother. She is understandably upset with us."

Lady Nora knew, of course, that Ariane being part of the commo link and the source of the power for it, would quite naturally monitor all conversations and transmissions. (Perhaps, I thought distractedly, that was one more ingredient to pour into the pot of simmering resentments: Ariane was always *there.* Almost a part of me.) But Lady Nora wasn't a high-chinned Great Vegan for nothing. She said, like a queen, "I am sorry, my dear Ariane"—and one knew that she wasn't in the *least* sorry—"but my son provokes me." And then the feminine flick with the knife, the trick of queen or coho-girl: "Of course if you could ever have a son yourself, you would understand this better, my dear."

Mercifully, Ariane did not reply.

Through the holographic screen came the faint sounds of muffled funeral drums, and I thought for a moment more about Gret and how—even as he lay dying (for he must have known he would not last long), he sent away Erit, his companion-friend-sister-wife—*everything*—to Gonlan, to serve his friends and "masters," the Rhad. He had sent Erit and he had begun a plan for me, and all the while he must have felt the long, long life slipping away from him. But he had thought of me, of my family, of the Rhadan folk among whom he had lived so long, of all the inhabitants of the Empire. His concern had been for us and those who would die if Marissa's *Death Three* were not found and rendered harmless. That thought made it a bit easier to stand against my mother's scathing attacks on my self-confidence, which continued unabated by her grief or mine or all Rhada's.

"Admiral Morag has been here, Kier," Lady Nora said, striking with her secondary armament. (It had always been easier to face my mother when I understood that she thought and fought like a soldier, with her friends and family and all the common people of Rhada as the unruly sometime-enemy.)

When I did not respond, she said, "She told me that there is still time to keep your infractions of the Fleet regulations within her jurisdiction. Provided that you return to Rhada at once."

"What else, Mother?"

"Ariane will be disciplined as well."

"What else?"

"The foreigner will be surrendered to the Navigators, naturally."

"Naturally," I said. "What will become of her?"

"She will be examined by the priesthood. It is obvious the warlocks can't pry information from her."

That I found interesting. My battlefield opponent had let slip a bit of possibly pertinent information. "Why is that, Lady?"

"Is she aboard, Ariane?"

So the information wasn't offered gratis. A bit for a bit.

Fair enough. It was like a skirmish by patrols ahead of the main force. The authorities must already know the girl was aboard. What I wanted to know was whether or not they were aware that she was from the Cloud and from the past.

"She is here," I said.

"The girl is a mutation," Lady Nora said, and I could see her shiver with xenophobia. "Apparently, she has a way of turning pain or pressure back on anyone who touches her. I gather some impatient warlocks got rather badly shocked. That was why she was being put into isolation when you took her. The precautions were not complete."

Well, that was a near evaluation of Marissa Tran Wyeth's peculiar powers. Close enough.

Lady Nora made a sudden flanking attack. "The Royalists have been sending messengers ever since yesterday, Kier. If you brought the girl here, to Rhada, and turned her over to the Rhadan priesthood—you'd put a fly in the eye of Sokolovsky. Our people would love you for it."

"I don't think you understand the danger, Mother. I can't explain it to you if you keep trying to turn what is happening into some sort of political coup for the family."

I subvocalized a question to Ariane, asking her how she and Marissa were coming with their effort to synthesize from the Magellanic girl's memory the attack plan for *Death Three*. Ariane beamed back an irritated reply that they were going as swiftly as the girl's "practically human" brain could function. (Maybe Ariane had a touch of racial prejudice, too?)

"And Erit?" I asked.

Ariane said, "She is in present isolation. She wished it so."

Knowing the habits of the Vulk, I surmised that Erit, now secluded in one of our auxiliary pods, would resume the mourning pose and remain so for hours, perhaps even days. During this time she would indulge in meditation, self-renewal, and a pattern of "prayer" so deep as to be almost coma-inducing. Regardless of the urgency of our need, she could do nothing else. Nor could we establish a

Triad with Marissa to plumb the depths of her subconscious memory. Two Vulk were vital to the experience. So we were effectively handicapped as well as grieved by the death of the old Vulk on the planet's surface. When Gret's great heart stopped, much of our power to act was lost.

Lady Nora was still speaking from the holograph. "—disappointment to me and to our family's supporters here on Rhada—"

This was nothing but a holding action. I began to grow suspicious. Lady Nora was never wordy or repetitious without a reason. But I was too firmly schooled and gently reared to break off a conversation with a noblewoman of the Empire—who also happened to be my mother and the hereditary first lady of Rhada.

"—I see that doesn't move you. Well, I am at the end of my resources, trying to make you see reason. If Erit is with you, I am shamed for what you have made her do and for what is worse, the thing you are making her do now—keeping her from Gret—"

"Gret is dead, Mother," I said in a flat voice. "And Erit is in mourning. There is no point in going on with this—"

"Wait. You were always a good boy, Kier, a faithful son and a Rhad. If you won't listen to me, then listen to someone wiser than I—" That false humility *had* to be a last resort, I thought. But I knew what would come next. The appeal to conscience, respect for a dear friend, ambition, and patriotism having failed, there remained only the church.

As an historian I have always had deep respect for the Order of Navigators. They kept knowledge alive through the Dark Time and piloted the starships when men imagined they could throw a stone across the galaxy. But the Order had outlived its usefulness—that was my inner conviction. The group that once guarded the guttering flame of science with their lives against the darkness had served its purpose. We no longer needed the Theocracy of Algol and its cloisters. Science was, or should be, open to all. We no longer needed the spiritual guidance and psychological guile of an isolated priesthood. Just as space navigation was no longer a monopoly of the Order's, so must all monopolies be broken. We had no use in our time for a priestly elite or for an Inquisition. The noble Order of Navigators, like all institutions that outlive their own time, was in danger of becoming rigid, destructive, and fanatical as its power diminished.

My mother knew this as well as, or possibly better than, I did. After all, I learned it from her. Therefore, I was aghast to see her joined in the holographic sphere by a cowled Navigator. But not just *any* Navigator, or even a Rhadan priest. The stone face that appeared beside Lady Nora belonged to Nav Peter, whom I had left lying in an undignified sprawl amid the ruins of Marissa Tran Wyeth's hospital room in Gonlanburg.

The Navigator made a sign of the Star and pierced me with the burning eyes of a fanatic. His face was granite-gray, and even his robes seemed to be dusted with gray, so that he seemed carved from common rock, the embodiment of his Zealot creed.

"My son," he intoned. "You have been guilty of grievous sin."

I had not heard anyone say the word "sin" like that since my childhood. It wasn't just wrong-doing that was implied there, but *sin* in the ancient sense: the crime of knowledge-seeking, of building in the darkness, of striving to raise the curtain on life a bit and search out the stars. That was the sort of sin the early Navigators talked about during the terrible time of the Interregnum, and that was exactly the sort Nav Peter meant now.

"I regret having struck you, Nav," I said respectfully. "It was without personal animosity, believe me."

"The indignities heaped on my person do not matter, Starkahn," the priest said. "The peril to your immortal soul does."

I had reached the degree of enlightenment that questions the existence of such things as immortal souls, but the fire-eyed Navigator was very convincing.

"The female you found in the void is an abomination and must be put to the Question, Starkahn. The Order is her proper guardian—"

The way he spoke of the Question made one think of the rack and the boot; what would actually happen to Marissa if she fell into the hands of the clergy would be far less physically violent than that. But if they questioned her and angered her or frightened her, and if the Magellanic Mutation (as it surely would) projected her emotions to them, their precarious hold on secular objectivity would shatter, and they would *treat* her as "an abomination."

This would be a sorry enough happening for me to contemplate (for I was swiftly growing rather fond of the alien girl); but more importantly it would be fatal in the search for knowledge about the machine we had taken to calling by its Magellanic name—too appropriate!—of *Death Three.*

It was, in fact, what all this was about. *And, therefore,* I thought suddenly, *why am I being harangued by a Navigator in this way? We can't possibly agree on anything, and surely everyone down on Rhada knows this. Then why am I standing here listening to talk about abominations, and immortal souls and whether or not Algol (or more likely a grim monastery in Syrtis Major on Mars) was the proper place for Marissa? They* knew *I wouldn't surrender her now, not after defying my family, the Grand Fleet, and all common sense to get her. They why all this? Why?*

A tiny cold bead formed in the pit of my stomach. It grew very swiftly, together with a surpassing contempt for my gullibility and empty-headedness.

I subvocalized to Ariane, "Check the interference along the commo beam. Are we being tracked by our transmissions?"

Instantly (or at least very swiftly, for Ariane was doing three things at once now, while maintaining our high orbit), the holograph image divided. In one section my mother and Nav Peter could still be seen and heard. In the other I had a view of space along the curving path of an orbital injection trajectory that roughly followed our line of sight transmissions to Rhada.

Coming fast was the unmistakable bulk of an Imperial starship of the Fleet.

General Nora Veg-Rhad's main force, wholly committed, was coming on, while idiot Sublieutenant Kier Veg-Rhad (who should be broken to private or lower if possible) stood babbling like a nitwit to a fanatic Navigator.

I burned with shame and anger, but I managed to say politely to Lady Nora over the shoulders of Nav Peter's holographic image, "Forgive me, honorable Lady, for interrupting the priest. But we are leaving *now!*" To Ariane I shouted, *"Break us out of orbit, fast!"*

One sometimes forgets how fast is *fast* to an ADSPS cyborg. The sudden G-load sent me spinning against the edge of the manual control console. The stars in the holograph blurred, shifted, streaked, and grouped in their familiar sphere as we went instantly translight. Then the stars mingled with another kind of exploding stars as I caromed off the console, across the floor to the hydraulic stanchion holding my pod, which I encountered squarely with the top of my thick skull. After that, there was peaceful darkness.

Chapter Twelve

A lifetime devoted to war has taught me that while terror and destruction have their place in successful conquest, total *terror and* total *destruction do not. When war is waged simply for the sake of revenge, it becomes meaningless.*

> Attributed to Glamiss of Vyka, circa 6000 GE
> (founder of the Second Stellar Empire)

History has often times failed to record the anomalous fact that its course is regularly changed by the actions of a small, relatively powerless group of individuals. It has happened many times in the past; it surely will happen many times again in the future.
Nav Julianus Mullerium, *The Age of the Star Kings*, middle Second Stellar Empire period

I awoke in the slightly gelatinous air of my pod that indicated Ariane was under heavy acceleration. In the thick fluid around me, I could smell the faintest strange odor of perfume—no, not that, nothing so artificial. It was the scent of a woman's skin and the clean smell of her hair. I drifted in a limbo of pleasure. My head was throbbing a bit, but I scarcely felt it. Someone was stroking my forehead with infinite gentleness. It was as though my body were drifting through a warm universe from planet to pink planet.

I opened my eyes and saw the silver-eyed girl leaning over me. "Good," she said softly. "You are all right."

I caught her hand and held the back of it against my cheek. Yes, it was she. Delicious. I had never felt so warm and tender and loving toward—

Ariane's voice exploded out of the encephalophone contacts at my head. "Kier! Wake up!"

Startled, I glanced at the instrument telltales on the rise of the pod before my eyes. Our speed was four kilolights: very nearly Ariane's max. Our direction was on course for Sagittarius through Delphinus, and we were taking full evasive action, dropping false target drones, radiating almost not at all, and carrying a full charge in all offensive and defensive weapons. Ariane was on full battle alert with her sensors extended to the very limit of their range. It would take time to track us by following her ionization trail. But track us they would.

I looked at Marissa and asked, "How long have I been out?"

"You were only unconscious for a short time. A mild concussion when you struck your head. You should have been inside the pod before you gave the order to leave orbit."

Did I detect a slightly chiding note in her speech? With her old-fashioned Anglic accent, it was hard to be sure. But it sounded to me as though she were, indeed, telling me (with a patient shake of her pretty head) that I had behaved recklessly.

I squinted at the chronometer. It showed that nearly a full ES day had passed since I spoke to my mother from orbit around Rhada. I sat up and mentioned that.

The Magellanic girl assumed an expression that was, God help me, as familiar as my own in a mirror. I had never seen it on *her* face, of course, but I had on my mother's and on the face of almost every woman I have ever known— even including Ariane, who strictly speaking doesn't even *have* a face. It was the expression a female assumes when she begins to manage a hapless male's existence because, dear and brave boy that he may be, he is, after all, only a *man*.

She said, "We thought it best you get some rest. You are overtired, and when we find the *Death*, you will need all your strength. So Ariane—" It was "Ariane" now. No horror and shock at dealing with a fifteen-ton cyborg. No wonder the captain of the Magellanic communes chose women to be Watchers on the great ships. They were *so adaptable*.

Marissa went on. "Ariane let you sleep until we had something for you to do."

That bland assumption of female power left me speechless. I had begun recently to worry about whether or not there was something about *me* that caused this power hunger among females. After this awakening, I was sadly certain of it.

"Did you reconstruct the attack plan?" I asked.

"As well as may be. There could be many errors. No one dreamed, when the *Deaths* were launched, that the Watcher would have any reason to study the attack plan. Erit has touched my mind with hers. How can they do that, Kier? It is so clean and clear, so much more *controlled* than the way of the Cloud people." She didn't wait for an answer: perhaps knowing I could give none, being only an ordinary human male. She said, "Erit has left off grieving."

At least in *that*, I knew she was wrong. The Vulk, might be awake and functioning. But her grief would never leave her—not until the day she joined Gret in that stone sepulcher on the lands of the Rhad.

"Erit has looked into my memory. She says that without Triad she cannot be certain, for my memories are not truly hers. But she *assumes* that we have very nearly worked out an intercept."

I stood and rubbed my aching head. The pod instruments indicated a surging four kilolight speed and a helical search pattern. I shouted irritably for Ariane to make a holograph for me. I was ready to take command of my illegal mission now if the females didn't mind.

To her credit let it be said that Ariane knows when to be humble. At least she knows when to *assume* humility. She showed me the navigational holograph as ordered. With Marissa at my side, I studied the smoky sphere of space before me. The stars were more thickly found in this region. Our course was taking us across our own spiral arm of the galaxy toward the spiral that extended here into Sagittarius. Deep in the Archer's sector lay a familiar type G star, Sol. The sun of Earth, cradle of the Empire. It was still far away, days' travel at our present speed. But the silent implications of our location and our apparent course were chilling.

If we were tracking *Death Three* by memory and deduction and we were right, I began to wish that the Imperial cruiser that Lady Nora's friends had sent after us at Rhada, and which had very nearly caught us in orbit, had actually done so. Then the responsibility would cease to be mine, and I would have nothing but a court martial to worry about.

I said, "I thought the *Death* would go from Delphinus deeper into the galactic center."

Marissa shook her head. I could feel that she had herself under rigid control. Very little of her emotional surge came through to me. But it was obvious she didn't want to tell me the answer to the questions she knew were coming.

"What was the projected course?" I asked.

"I am not certain."

"Of course you aren't certain. But you and Ariane plotted a hypothetical attack plan, and Erit probed you. What did the three of you decide the *Death* would do?"

"We cannot be certain, Kier—"

"I know that, Marissa. *But answer the question.*"

"We think the *Death* will circle back into Sagittarius."

I felt a sinking sensation. "You can't be sure of that."

"No, we can't be. But we made some deductions, I remembered some things—and there has been another sighting."

"After Sigma Libra?"

The girl nodded, her silver eyes lowered.

"Where?" I asked, feeling sick.

She raised her head and spoke softly to Ariane, who shifted the navigational holograph to the celestial north, above the galactic ecliptic. A super-bright star burned in the darkness, expanding even as I watched, and showing— at this stellar distance—a distinctly spherical shape. Supernova.

"Ariane," I said. "Which is it?"

"That's the strange part of it, Kier. It hasn't even a name, only a number in the New Galactic Catalogue. No planets. NGC 6698."

"Could it have been a natural phenomenon?"

"No," Ariane said flatly. "The star was recently surveyed. Eighteen ES months ago, in fact, by Lieutenant Commander Riso Bel-Koryzibsky and Deela Cyb-ADSPS 217. It showed not one characteristic of instability. The nova was triggered by a massive attack on the stellar photosphere. The *Death Three* without a doubt."

"You've made a plot projection?"

"By helical extension, the *Death* can be in solar space within a week or, on the next sweep, in two and a half months. I *don't* think we have to worry about the latter date, do you?"

"Could it possibly be earlier?"

"Not if the attack program included inhibitions against overusing the main propulsion systems."

Marissa said, "That's true. The *Deaths* were all built to take the most economical orbits. Fighting range was important to the designers—and since they are practically impregnable, speed intra-galaxy isn't."

"But the positronic controls are damaged." I said.

"We don't know that for sure," Marissa said.

"Of course we do. Why else would it attack NGC 6698? There's nothing there. There never has been. The farther the *Death* gets from its point of activation in Delphinus, the less rational—if we can use such a word in connection with a doomsday machine—it becomes."

"Nothing will impair its fighting capacities," Marissa warned.

I looked at the silvery eyes in that finely made, handsome face. I wondered if she were actually, in some perverse way, proud of the hell ship she had brought to the main galaxy? It was probably true—she was mostly human, and such self-destroying pride could be very much a part of our human makeup.

"It was programmed for Earth," I said quietly. "You knew that all along."

The girl nodded slowly. "Earth was the home, the hub, of the Eugenicist movement. . . ."

"It is also the home of the entire race," I said.

She looked at me with mute appeal. Then she said, "Out there—in the Cloud—I don't know how to explain it to you. It seemed *right*. We had cause to do as we did, and we were all *together*—"

"That is the key, of course," I said.

"The key?"

"To unlock the box full of evils that set you on your way, so arrogant, so filled with moral outrage and a sense of having been wronged that you'd destroy all human life in the galaxy if you could. You had that wonderful feeling of *community*, and so you *knew* you were right." I felt sick and I suppose I showed it.

"It was right, then," she said hopelessly.

I shook my head. "It is wrong now, and it was just as wrong then. Revanchism. Mass murder. Genocide. Not nearly so noble an effort when we call it by its right name."

"A moment, Starkahn." Erit stood in the open valve, the soft light shining on her eyeless face and sensitive mouth. "We may all die together, so it is well to treat with one another fairly and with honesty. Marissa Tran Wyeth has done this. So must you. We are dealing with a case of *attempted* genocide, *attempted* racial murder. The verdict of history is something we must let the future pronounce. Our job, we four, is to stand together and fight. We are the only ones who can do it. Otherwise, we would have called in the Grand Fleet—isn't that so, Starkahn?"

"I think so," I said. I really wasn't sure. The wild adventure, the impossible fight, still appealed to me. Was I being a child? Playing a game and gambling with the lives of my friends, with the lives of billions?

"Kier!"

It was Ariane. I felt the lurch of speed increasing. I couldn't imagine where she was finding the power to surpass a four thousand times light-speed velocity, but she was.

"What have you found?"

"Ionization trail, Kier. Massive. The *Death* has traveled this way."

"How long ago?"

"No less than a day ago. No more than a month. That is the best I can do. But I can plot the direction of the trail."

I waited. Presently, the cyborg reported in a carefully controlled and neutral voice, "An extension of the helix penetrates Sagittarius in the Province of Tellus, the District of Lemuri. Is that near enough?"

"Too near," I said heavily. "The star nearest the trail, then?"

"Sol."

"Yes. Thank you." There was nothing else to say, nothing else to do but continue the slowest sort of pursuit there was—the stern chase. Ariane was faster by a factor of one hundred than the ancient and clumsy starship, but the distances were so immense that we could very well arrive in solar space too late and find only the tenuous fiery gases of an expanding planetary nebula—

And among the disintegrating molecules would be the history of man, from his beginnings among the hominids of the old continents, through Galileo and Shakespeare and Spinoza and the great ancients, to Faraday and Einstein and

Gagarin and Aldrin and Armstrong, to St. Emeric and Nav Kynan and—

Oh, the list was endless, timeless, as man was timeless! But the black starship could bring most of it to an end, destroying as it did so the heart of a mighty Second Stellar Empire of man.

For an *attempt* at genocide and mass murder, it seemed to have a dismayingly good chance of succeeding.

Chapter Thirteen

Where will it end, I ask, good people?
Grim people, cold people, warlike people, hateful
humans!
Some day it will end, you know—
The finger of God will point at you from the sky—
          Torquas XIII (called The Poet),
          18th Vykan Galacton, 6212 GE-6252 GE

When asked what troops he considered the best, Glam-
iss is said to have replied: "Those which are victo-
rious." The Rhad say he spoke of them.
Nav Julianus Mullerium, *The Age of the Star Kings,*
middle Second Stellar Empire period.

Yes, I have a doctrine in battle, and I recommend it
to my descendants for as long as they follow the war-

man's trade: When weary and dispirited—attack.
When outnumbered and outflanked—attack. When
faced with impossible odds and certain defeat—at-
tack. Attack, attack, attack!

    Attributed to Aaron the Devil,
    first Star King of Rhada, circa 6000 GE (?),
    early Second Stellar Empire or Interregnal period

We followed the ion trail left by the great starship for eight
Earth Standard Days. The archaic design of the engines and
their immense size made Ariane's task of tracking it through
the end of Sagittarius reasonably easy. So far the trail had
not been detected by any units of the Grand Fleet, but it
was only a matter of time, for we were now penetrating the
Inner Marches: the center, not of the galaxy proper, but of
the most densely populated areas, the region of the stars
nearest Earth. In this province of the Empire lay Alpha
Centaurus, Barnard's Star, Wolf 359, and, dominating the
darkness with its size and brilliance, Sirius—at this distance
a clear visual double. Around these stars revolved the ancient worlds, the planets of scholars and libraries, laboratories and universities. These Inner Worlds were the first
colonized when man liberated himself from the tyranny of
Sol. They formed, in most ancient times, the heartlands of
the First Empire (hence their Dawn Age names). Now they
lay under their own varied skies, somnolent, academic,
untroubled by war or conflict of any sort since Glamiss the
Magnifico's time. And it was into this peaceful region of
space that the *Death Three* was now moving.

    Ariane pointed out quite properly that if the *Death* was
intercepted by any major Fleet unit, the scenario would be
completely predictable: All capital starships of the Grand
Fleet were commanded by noble, titled commanders from
the great warman families of the Empire. Since the Empire
had been at peace for three hundred years, they would be
anxious to provoke some military incident that might produce a victory, glory, and Imperial attention. Yet they were

all inexperienced in any sort of serious ship-to-ship combat. Added to this would be the massive power of the *Death*'s weaponry and the fact that the vessel's positronic program banks were damaged. For a starship of the Grand Fleet to engage the *Death* would be rather like a small boy with a sharp stick attacking an armored, mounted warman about to go berserk.

We could not receive any radio transmissions as long as we remained in the translight speed ranges, so it was impossible to know whether or not the ionic swath of the doomsday vessel across the Inner Marches had yet been discovered. But it was inevitable that it should be, and soon. We had to overtake the great ship before it committed mass murder.

The relationship that rapidly developed between Ariane and Marissa Tran Wyeth was a strange one, or so it seemed to me (though Erit assured me that it was quite a normal state of arrested hostility—the sort often found between two strong-minded women). But once the shock of realizing that the ship was a cyborg, and a female cyborg at that, had worn off, Marissa accepted Ariane with more toleration than Ariane offered the Magellanic girl. So it seemed to me, in any case. Perhaps the reason for it was that Marissa, who had been trained (so *long* ago!) as a scientist for her duties as Watcher, admired Ariane's abilities—almost in spite of herself. Erit suggested that the fact of her being human (at least in the important particulars) while Ariane weighed fifteen metric tons might also have something to do with it. "You, Starkahn, are the only man she has had a chance to become acquainted with since her awakening," Erit said.

These considerations, however, seemed likely to remain academic. Of primary importance was the problem of what we were to do if and when we succeeded in tracking down the *Death Three*. The simple act of getting anywhere near the monster could quite easily result in our being blasted into hot vapor. And, if we should be permitted within range and allowed to try to put Marissa back on her ship, we had no assurance that the mechanisms aboard would work as their designers had intended—ten thousand years ago.

In all, our situation was tense and not calculated to fill us with confidence. By this time we were listed as deserters from the Grand Fleet (surely the *first* time a *ship* had defected). The fact of my being a Rhad noble (whose mother plagued the Republic with royalist plots and bothers) was cause for some alarm among the more timid in the Imperial civil service, I was sure. Then Ariane's "ancestry" was probably stirring up old memories of the great cyborg rebellions of First Empire times. That couldn't be good. In addition to this, we had a Vulk with us. Time out of mind anti-Vulkism had plagued the Empires—First *and* Second. And finally, Nav Peter and his fanatics must surely be spreading the word among the faithful that an "abomination" from the Cloud was leading us all astray and into damnation. Meanwhile, *Death Three*'s damaged brain muddled its way through the long-ago imprinted and programmed attack plan intended to kill Eugenicists and adherents of the Raschilid Dynasty.

I lounged disconsolately in my pod, with the curving surfaces around me polarized to let the night come through. Erit and Marissa were beyond the open valve to the bridge: I could hear their murmured talk. Erit was being very kind to the girl from the Cloud, and in return Marissa was trying to describe the sort of life she had led in the communes of Magellan. Erit, being a Vulk and nonmechanical, probably thought the life of the Magellanics sad and lacking in hope or dignity. But she would never say so. Her only comment was to repeat what she had said before: that perhaps the present-day inhabitants of the Cloud had turned to more rewarding pursuits than vengeance.

I looked across the interstellar night at mighty Sirius, blue-white, flooding the darkness with diamond light. We were moving in a steady search-spiral around the ion traces left by the *Death*. Our speed was just sublight now, for we wanted to intercept any radio traffic in this district of Sagittarius.

The result was a normal-looking sky, beautifully dusted with distant stars, alight with the nearer suns, and touched with the softness of deep space: black as raven's wings.

Ariane said, "I have been thinking, Kier." I could feel the touch of her affection for me. The E-phones were not as effective in transmitting emotions as the Magellanic Mutation, but somehow Ariane got the message across. We had been together a long time. "This thing we are doing could be—very likely will be—the end of us."

"I have been thinking the same thing, Ari," I said.

"Even if we succeed—which is very doubtful—the powers will want to separate us. We have broken every rule."

"Very nearly," I said with a thoughtful smile.

"Are you in love with that girl?"

I squirmed uncomfortably, but I thought about it—faced it for the first time. "I don't know," I said finally.

"I think you are," Ariane said.

I pursed my lips and looked at the vista beyond the pod walls.

"I am not a human woman, Kier," Ariane said. "That does not mean I am without feelings. I am not—as she put it—a robot."

"I know that," I said.

"I simply want you to know that I understand what is happening," the cyborg said, and I thought of the way people who didn't have this sort of symbiotic tie to another kind of living being looked at SW people and said, "Those pilots and their cyborgs," not understanding that there are many faces of love.

I was at a loss for something to say. To be parted from Ariane would be to separate myself into two parts: each part to remain alone from then on, for as long as I lived. It was frightening and terribly sad.

"What happens will happen," Ariane said, with cyb fatalism.

I wanted to promise her that nothing would ever change in our relationship, but I couldn't do that, not to Ariane, who had shared a hundred adventures and pleasures with me.

Marissa came through the valve and stood at my pod. She could feel what I was feeling, and she touched my hand gently and said, "I have come a long way to bring trouble to you and yours, Kier of Rhada. I am sorrier than I can say."

"You did what your people trained you to do, Marissa," I said.

"Have I done more than that? Have I come between you and your cyborg?" The silver eyes held that dark sadness they sometimes did, and I felt torn between an old loyalty and—was Ariane right?—love?

A shock of discovery ran through Ariane's extended search systems. Even before she alerted me, I felt it through the encephalophone contacts. Marissa said,"What is it?"

Ariane replied, through the grid speakers, so that Erit and Marissa could know what had aroused her, "Contact in the S-band. Extreme range."

"Fleet signals?" I asked.

"No. I'll give you a holograph." She materialized a cone of space in the pod and blanked out the walls. Sirius and its companion hung in the air of the pod, and I could make out the three largest of the great star system's thirty planets. There could have been something at the center of the holograph, something that should not have been there, but we were too far away to get a clear return.

"Range?"

"Two parsecs. That's approximate. An hour at two kilolights. Maybe a bit more. I am computing," Ariane said. Gone was the wistful cyborg. This was an ADSPS cyborg performing her function.

Erit glided noiselessly into the bridge. "Have we found the *Death?*"

"I think so," I said. "In Sirius." I turned to Marissa.

"Was the Sirius system part of the attack program?"

Marissa shook her head.

"Then perhaps it is not the *Death*," Erit suggested.

"I can make a measurement now," Ariane said. "Wait one." While she sent out the translight pulses, she said, "It is orbiting, but the orbit is eccentric. It is under power."

I waited anxiously. The S-band radar, sparkling with strong stellar emissions from Sirius's blue-white photosphere, was giving no steady indications. There was obviously something there, but the blip was unsteady, scruffy in the aurora of the stellar wind that flared out of the giant star.

Ariane said, "Dead mass is 1,000,906,098,006 metric tons. It is the *Death*."

The breath whistled from my lips. It was an expression of mingled relief and dread. We had found the monster again. Now what did we do about it?

"It shouldn't be in Sirius at all," Marissa said. "That means the programming has broken down completely."

"Then Earth, at least, is safe for the time being," Erit said.

"But it might also mean the *Death* will refuse to accept its Watcher," Marissa said.

I looked at her bleakly. "It might mean that, of course." To Ariane I said, "Close the range. Hold at a mega-K."

"Yes, Starkahn," the cyborg replied. "You can't stay in the pods, so everyone take a gravigen tablet." A dispenser extruded from the console.

I swallowed the capsule and watched while Erit and Marissa did the same. Then I said, "Into space armor, Marissa. Let's do it now." There was no armor on board small enough to suit Erit, so I secured her within the control pod and closed the latches. To Ariane I gave orders that Erit was to be ejected if we were disabled by any of the *Death*'s light weapons. A hit by heavier offenses would vaporize us and sterilize a few hundred thousand cubic miles of space in our vicinity. There was no point in dwelling on that possibility.

Marissa and I, bulky in our EV gear now, had little to do while Ariane tracked and closed. She gave us a running commentary on all that was happening outside, but for the moment there was nothing we could do but wait. I was haunted by the thought that the *Death* intended to destroy Sirius. The other stars it had imploded were obscure bodies, unknown to most of mankind. But Sirius—the mighty Dog Star—was a familiar feature of Earth's night sky. A nova of that magnitude was beyond imagining.

"What are the defensive systems?" I asked Marissa.

"I don't know how they function," the girl said, her voice metallic in my headset. "They are force-field variants. They are keyed to my molecular structure. They will reject anyone else—that is all I am sure of."

"When and how were they imprinted? When you came aboard?"

"When I left the capsule," she said.

I felt a sinking sensation in my belly. By the holy Star, I had done it again. Careless, thoughtless, *stupid*. Why hadn't I thought this through before we began this insane chase, I wondered?

Because it was becoming sickeningly clear suddenly— the glaring mistake in my reasoning. She had *told* me before and I hadn't listened, hadn't realized the significance of what she had said and what she was saying *now*.

The defenses of the black starship had been inactive during the long flight from the Cloud and during its millennial wait in Delphinus. They probably devoured power, and there was no need to activate them until the ship began its attack plan. So logically enough, the defenses were activated when the Watcher awoke. *But the girl had been awakened in Gonlan and not, as the Magellanics intended, aboard the starship*.

And, therefore, the starship would *not* regard Marissa as a Watcher. It would not accept her. To the primitive systems of the ship, she was bound to be identified as another enemy.

So all of this: taking Marissa from the warlocks, tracking the starship across the galaxy, closing with it now—all this was a hopeless, gratingly useless gesture. She could not possibly get aboard.

I told the others my thoughts, and for a long while we simply sat in stunned silence. The logic of it was inescapable—and deadly.

If Ariane had been a computer or a robot (as so many people of our time thought of her), she would have seen the problem at the outset. But she was a cyborg, a cybernetic *organism*, and, as such, as fallible as any human. Nor could the nonmechanical Vulk have been expected to foresee the check. No, the fault was mine and no one else's.

I knew then what I must do. There is an ancient saying among my mother's people, the Great Vegans. In one form or another, it is familiar to all the people of the main galaxy. *The Star King is father to his people.* I was a poor excuse for a star king, and poorer still for a father. But there was a single chance, and I must take it.

I said, "Ariane. Remember when we first encountered this thing in Delphinus—and I went aboard?"

"I remember, Starkahn."

"You said something to me while I was in the life-support chamber. You said that something was happening to the ship."

"Yes. The cores began to function *after* you'd gone aboard."

"Isn't it possible the sensors took *me* for the Watcher?"

"That seems a farfetched chance, Kier," Erit said.

I looked at Marissa. Her gleaming eyes regarded me from the bulk of the suit helmet. "Is it possible, Marissa?"

"I don't know, Kier," the girl said.

"How selective can life sensors be? How selective would it be necessary to make them? After all, the builders didn't expect anyone *ever* to be aboard the *Death* but a Watcher. Surely they wouldn't be able to differentiate between one human being and another."

"But Marissa is not a human being. Not in the same way you are," Ariane protested.

"Near enough," I said, with an assurance I didn't feel.

"And the ship began to move after I had boarded it. I barely had time to get off before it went translight. You remember, Ariane. We even tried to hold it with a torpedo, but it was too far along with the core lighting. It just went." I drew a deep breath and said positively, "It took *me* for its Watcher."

"That is a dangerous assumption, Kier," Ariane said.

"It is the only one we can make," I said. "I'll go aboard again."

"Kier!" Ariane said sharply. "I have a Fleet contact." She holographed the expanding space where the black starship curved into Sirius's inner zone. An Imperial battleship and three cruisers had materialized out of translight mode. Their intentions were unmistakable. They might have had battleflags flying, so obvious was their intention to attack the giant.

"The commo station on Sirius Fifteen has been sending out a distress call. They must have detected the *Death* coming in," Ariane said.

Marissa looked at me with frightened eyes. "S-Fifteen is the outermost habitable planet in the system," I said. "We are approaching from the night side, so we can't see it. But they must have radar contact with the *Death*."

Marissa's voice was horrified. "Are there people on the planet, Kier? Many people?"

"It is a water world," Ariane said. "Larger than Earth. Seven large islands in a planetary ocean."

"But people? Cities?"

"A population of seventeen millions," I said flatly. "Would the *Death* attack a planetary body?"

"Yes," Marissa said. "It could do that."

I turned back to the holograph. The battleship and its englobing cruisers were moving at sublight speeds, but they were driving hard to intercept. A gallant gesture—and a futile one.

"Ariane," I said. "Tell those ships who we are, and say that they are to veer off." I drew a deep breath and then gave the order, "Close in on the *Death*. I am boarding her again."

In that moment, for the first time in my life (and quite possibly the last, I realized), I felt like the Starkahn of Rhada.

Chapter Fourteen

The Book of Warls says that there are demons in the Cloud which one may see in the southern skies of Earth and that these demons lived on the Earth, and on Vyka, and on all the worlds of men. Now, I have been to Earth, and to Vyka, and to many worlds, and I find it most curious that the only demons I have met there are my fellow men.

> Attributed to Navigator Anselm Styr,
> burned for heresy at Biblios Brittanis,
> early Second Stellar Empire

The death of the Royal Vulk Gret, coming as it did when his participation in Triad with the Magellanic invader would have disclosed the impossibility of effective action against the marauding Death Three, is ironic. The truth, as the invader knew it, would have

*made any attempt to neutralize the great starship use-
less. But the Rhadan Starkahn, a precipitous youth,
did not discover until too late that the Magellanic's
presence could not quiet the threat, and so he acted
in a spirit of self-immolation. Thus, even in death,
the Vulk Gret served the state.*
  Vulk Varinius (Academician of the Council of
  Ministers, 625-870 New Galactic Era), *My People*,
  middle Confederate period

Once again I found myself in space approaching that great
metal planetoid. I had instructed Ariane to retreat to a thousand kilometers, and there, invisible to me, she matched
the *Death*'s orbit and waited.

At a distance of eight thousand kilometers, the night side
of the planet Sirius Fifteen blotted out a large part of the
sky. The double star lay behind the planet as seen from my
location, and I could clearly make out the star's diamond-
bright corona. It shimmered like an aurora, a vast stellar
wind of glowing particles that dimmed the more distant
stars.

In the bulky armor I felt hot and clammy. There was a
hard knot of real fear in my belly, for I fully expected to
be met with a blast of destroying defensive energies as I
approached the Magellanic vessel. Marissa had briefed me
as well as she could concerning the rudimentary controls
available within the ship. They consisted mainly of several
methods of reducing the power inputs to the various systems
within the giant: defensive armaments and propulsion. The
offensive weapons were far beyond Marissa's comprehen-
sion, having been designed by the malign genius of an entire
civilization's most brilliant minds.

As I approached the massive ship, I was struck once
again by its derelict appearance. The projecting cones of
the intersystem drive, the extensions of the main cores, still
scintillated faintly with the residual energies it had expended
to slow from faster-than-light speeds to a mere crawl—the
twenty-seven thousand kilometers per ESH needed to es-

tablish an eccentric orbit around the watery planet below. In that flickering glow I could see that the knobs and protrusions I had noticed on the ship's surface previously were now fully extended, and the blunt muzzles of energy projectors, rhomboidal in shape and alien to the eye, projected far above the black, curving surface of the ship's skin. It was difficult to be certain in the dimness, but it did seem to me that grids that appeared to be search radar were scanning rapidly, bobbing and weaving like fans as they probed space all around. I wondered, dry-mouthed, if one of those hundreds of antennae were scanning *me*, sending its pulses down through the kilometers of circuitry to the addled positronic brain of the robot and asking whether or not the tiny mote it had discovered were a threat and should it spare a small portion of destruction to wipe it out. It was not a comforting notion.

I heard Ariane through the E-phone: "You are within six kilometers, Kier. I cannot detect any rise in radiation. Perhaps you are too small to be noticed."

I didn't believe that for a moment, and I didn't think the cyborg did. She said it for the same reason small children whistle when passing burial grounds at night.

"Have you been able to raise the battleship?" I asked. Ariane had sent pulses to the Imperial vessels before I went EV, but the range was great and the situation aboard the warships tense, I had no doubt. Our signals had apparently not been received—or they had not yet been passed through the absurdly complicated chain of command that has become deadly common practice in the Grand Fleet after all these years of peace.

"I am trying now. I've told them they must hold their position and under no circumstances attempt to attack because we have someone EV in the area of the *Death*."

Since Ariane's messages would contain our commo code identification symbols, there was no doubt the commander of the Imperial squadron would know *who* was extra vehicular near the marauder. That might slow them down some. If what I knew of high commanders in the Fleet held true in this case, the lord nobleman on the battleship's bridge would soon be burning up the long-range commo beacons with pleas for special instructions. Our Imperial officers did not reach flag rank by being rash.

I turned my attention once again to the great starship. The rhomboidal muzzles were moving—there was no doubt of it. They were training around so that those that were not masked by the bulk of the vessel were pointing at the planet— or at the star beyond. I felt a shivering terror mingled with a reluctant admiration for Marissa's people of the communes. What sort of men could, in a few short decades, develop a technology like this? And an understanding of stellar-phoenix reactions so complete that they could apply a mote of power in the right manner to puncture the photosphere and destroy the equilibrium of a star! What could such minds have done if they had devoted themselves to something other than revenge and weaponry? For that matter, the time scale was all wrong: perhaps in the millennia that had passed they *had* done just that and turned inward to explore their own galaxy—and others. And why was it that we in the main galaxy had only this messenger of death, launched thousands of years before, to speak for the communes of Magellan?

Was it possible my human mind was too rigid to really understand? Was it possible, for example, that *time* itself was something different outside the Milky Way? Did each galactic system have its own particular time flow? Perhaps Marissa wasn't a ten-thousand-year sleeper at all in her own environment of the Cloud. Perhaps the builders of the *Deaths* were still living— Perhaps— My mind spun with the vast and limitless options that would remain unanswered until more men and women make the long voyage—took, as Marissa said, the Long Death. And none of this would ever come to pass if the *Death Three* continued its destructive journey.

In this fight the stakes were nothing less than the future of man: peace and exploration of an increasingly wondrous universe—or very nearly everlasting war and fear of further incursions by "the demons of the Cloud" who seemed sprung from the pages of the ancient *Book of Warls*, black bible of the Interregnal warlocks.

The sun was rising. Not the sun, but Sirius, the brilliant double star of legend. It appeared in a scintillating flare of hot bright light over the dark horizon of Sirius Fifteen, the planet below. Its rays were turning "the wine-dark sea" of the ancients into a restless silver. The swirling clouds made a pattern that caught the red rays of the growing daylight and held them for a time. Then the inexorable motions of the celestial mechanics that governed the immense masses of star and planet caused them to move on in their long cycles, and far above, in the night of space beyond the stratosphere, the first white light struck the alien starship, and it seemed to take on form and substance, mass and dimension. I watched it and felt minute, miniscule, infinitesimal. What, I wondered, can one single man do against the ponderous and unthinking powers of the great beings involved? In my dread I was beginning to revert to the mysticism of the Rhad: we are thought a melancholy people, filled with barely contained wonder. Natural enough, I think, for a nation born on the edge of the known galaxy, with a window, as it were, on the truly infinite.

With its relatively dark companion at apastron, Sirius appeared to fill much of the sky, even though the first and nearest of the planetary companions revolved around the system at a distance of more than one hundred astronomical units. Sirius Fifteen's orbit lay a thousand times farther away from its primary than did the orbit of Neptune from Sol; yet so large was the great Dog Star that the planet below was subtropical—a paradise of islands and warm sea. On this lambent world lived seventeen millions of my fellow human beings—persons I had never seen, but who had suddenly, in my mind at least, become my brothers and sisters.

I touched the thruster controls and moved toward the *Death*. I was suddenly filled with a sense of fate. Perhaps

I was finally beyond ordinary fear.

Ariane said, "The battleship is the *Intrepid*, Captain Lord Chal Proc-Ouspensky commanding. He says he will hold his position for one hour—no longer. Also he says that we are under arrest and may not leave Sirius district without his express orders."

The marvelous way our noblemen's minds worked, I thought with a touch of hysteric gaiety. If they were tossing coins, they would contrive to have them land always on edge.

"Acknowledge his transmission, but tell him we do not accept his authority," I said. "We take our instructions directly from the Fleet Survey Wing. It won't stop him, but it will confuse and immobilize him for at least that hour."

"There is something else, Kier," Ariane said. "One of the cruisers is a Navigator's ship with a completely ecclesiastical crew. He will not speak for them. They are Zealots to a man."

"What ship?" I asked, dreading the answer.

"The *Glory of the Name* from the Theocracy. Navigator Peter commands her."

Of course, I thought. *It had to be.* The Zealots would insist on being in at the death of the *Death.* But his lack of understanding of what was involved here could be fatal to all of us. Nav Peter had never before seen the Magellanic vessel. His devil-ridden mind was too rigidly religious to conceive of such a craft being built without the sanction and blessing of the Order of Navigators. Now, what would the sight of the monster do to that irrational man's powers of reason?

"Can you relay me through to the *Glory*, Ariane?" I asked.

"If they will take a call. They may not choose to talk to a blasphemer and heretic."

"Try it anyway." As I exchanged messages with Ariane, I kept drawing cautiously closer to the *Death.* I was within five kilometers now, and the small of my back was tingling with warning messages, and the expectation of sudden blasting extinction.

So Nav Peter had joined the chase, and probably it was his authority as nuncio of the Theocracy that had brought poor Lord Ouspensky and his squadron to this deadly place. *Unfortunate man,* I thought drily. He should have had a good and simple life as lord of his estates in the Procyon worlds. Instead, he now commanded a small detachment of Imperial ships in imminent danger of vaporization.

I heard a harsh voice say in the E-phones: "This is the *Gloria Nomini,* heretic. Speak." Latin, I thought with irrational irritation. In this time and this place, *Latin.* A language dead even in the middle years of the Dawn Age. But these were the men who had kept knowledge alive through the Dark Time. For that, I owed them respect. Even such as the Zealots. I replied, "I hear you, Nav. I would speak with Peter of Syrtis."

"Then speak."

"Nav Peter," I said, as respectfully as I could under the circumstances, "I ask that you remain with the squadron and make no sudden moves. It could be extremely dangerous."

"The Order fears no dangers, heretic. The spirit of the Star is with us."

I racked my brain trying to think of some way to make even a minimal breakthrough of understanding with the fervid priest. It was vital. I remembered that the Zealots were probably the last adherents to what, in Nav Kynan of Rhada's time, was called the Stellar Heresy. In the middle years of the Empire's development, certain Navigators put forward the theory that stars were in and of themselves holy, and objects of veneration. The more extreme star worshipers propounded the hypothesis that the stars were not simply celestial bodies (and as such works of the Universal Spirit or God), but rather *aspects* of God: living, sentient beings. And just as the priests of the Dawn Age had wrangled to the point of bloodshed over "how many angels could dance

on the head of a pin," the Navigators of the early Empire
split into angry factions over the Stellar hypothesis, or as
some called it, the Stellar Heresy. If Nav Peter of Syrtis
were, in fact, a stellarite, then the destruction of a star was
the most heinous crime imaginable: not because it destroyed
the works of man, but because it was a direct assault on the
body and *person* of God Himself.

"You can see the danger on your own instruments, Nav,"
I said. "It is a starship from the Cloud. A vast vessel, but only
a ship. There is no religious question here. Let me—"

"Everything that happens is a religious matter, Starkahn,"
the priest's rasping voice went on, tense and near to hys-
terical rage. "Is there no end to your presumption?"

"Nav," I said, "there is no need for the Order to become
involved in this. It is a matter for the Fleet. I beg you, stand
clear and live."

"To threaten a Navigator of God is to risk damnation,
Kier of Rhada. Don't imagine your patrician birth will help
you in this."

The millennial prejudice of the humbly born for the noble
was in his words, and I realized that here was a basically
simple man, a peasant, with the power of the clergy (no,
of God, he thought) in his hands. The meek to humble the
mighty. The man born of the soil to put down the Starkahn.
It was too bitter, too sadly hopeless. I could not touch the
man's small nucleus of sanity. His prejudice and vaulting
arrogance were too great.

"I am not threatening you, Nav," I said. "Only let me
do what I must, and I will submit myself to an ecclesiastical
court on Rhada—on Mars, if you like! A court of damned
Zealots—!"

"Blasphemy and heresy. You bargain with God's will!"
In the darkness of a distant starfield I saw the familiar
scintillation of a starship's hull glowing with ionization. The
Navigator's ship was getting under way. I almost screamed
into the E-phone: *"Stay where you are, Peter! On peril of
all our lives, don't come closer!"*

"That abomination of demons has murdered stars. It must

submit to the Order or be destroyed," Nav Peter shouted.

Insanity. Religious fanaticism would be the end of us all here in the Sirian sky, I thought hopelessly. Now I could make out the shape of the Navigator's cruiser. It was patterned on the ancient vessels, so like the monster before me. Yes, insanity and irony. How bitter it was!

I pleaded as I rotated slowly in space like a miniature spaceship. "Nav Peter. Give me an hour. One hour, that I can try to board this thing and immobilize it—!"

"Do you think I will allow a heretic to grasp the demon's power? I excommunicate you, Kier of Rhada!" He cut off communications, and there was nothing in my E-phone but the hiss and crackle of stellar static from the blazing blue-white sun.

Ariane warned, "The Nav cruiser is under acceleration, Kier! Get away! I'm coming in to pick you up!"

"Ariane, no!"

A pale violet aurora formed around one of the Magellanic's projectors. It danced and shimmered and seemed to reach out toward me, as though the addled memory-bank that controlled it were confused, uncertain. Then it brightened to a flaring electric blue that tripped the selsium cells in my suit and snapped the screens down over my eyes. But the blazing pseudopod of force curved away from me and darted in a solid bolt of hellish light toward the Navigator's vessel. There was a white flash, a globule of sun-bright brilliance. It was soundless and all the more terrifying for its silence. And I saw the cruiser, a vast machine itself, bulge and distort as though the molecules of its fabric were bloating with impossible energies. Then it was gone in a swiftly expanding ball of hot gases.

I heard Ariane calling me, and I thought I heard even Marissa in the soundless confusion. A storm of radiation smashed violently against my armor, and I was spun over and over by the pressure of the light that was the by-product of the deadly explosion of the cruiser. I tumbled toward the dark ship, and in my fall I noticed with strange lucidity that the other projectors were dark, as though the strike against

Nav Peter's ship of priests had momentarily drained the defensive systems of power.

Below me lay the familiar black metal plain, studded with menacing projections. Then as I fell I saw the dark portal—the same open pit that I had ventured into what seemed an eternity ago in Delphinus. Without hesitation I triggered my suit thrusters, righted myself, and plunged into the Stygian darkness.

Chapter Fifteen

Good sense or reason must be better distributed than anything else in the world, for no man desires more of it than he already has.

> René Descartes, *Discourse on Method*,
> early Dawn Age

If a man succeeds in a dangerous enterprise, he is called a hero. If he fails, he may be called a fool— or not be called at all.

> St. Emeric of Rhada,
> Grand Master of Navigators,
> early Second Stellar Empire period

It was as though I were entrapped in a recurring dream. First came the suffocating darkness and then the long free fall "down" the open shaft toward the tiny chamber imbedded in the mass of nucleonic circuitry deep inside the great starship.

As I fell, my only contact with reality was Ariane's continuous calls on the E-phone. She had closed to within a perilous range, risking her own destruction and the death of Marissa and Erit, but her signals came through sharp and clear. She did not wait for any responses from me, but kept up a running commentary on what was happening outside the vessel.

"The *Intrepid* and the rest of the squadron are withdrawing to ten thousand kilometers. The fireball and the wreckage are still expanding. The Nav ship is completely destroyed."

Then: "The *Death* is moving. I am following. Speed is sublight. Direction is toward the planet."

And: "The energy level is rising. I can detect heavy ionization of subspace in the vicinity of the *Death*."

I struck the smooth wall of the shaft and went into a tumbling spin. The sensation jolted me into action, and I began to fly my armor with the thrusters. It seemed to me that the shaft was no longer than before, but I knew this was illusion. Yet the ship *was* moving. Inertia kept trying to smash me against the walls, and it took all my training with the armor to remain more or less in the middle of the shaft.

Ariane called: "I know you are conscious, Kier. I am receiving telemetry. But try to say what is happening to you."

I said through the encephalophone, "I am all right. I'm under control. I don't know whether or not the ship *let* me in. I may have made it because it was using power to destroy the Nav cruiser."

Then I sensed Marissa through the E-circuit. She said, "It took you for the Watcher. I am certain of it. There would never have been a power lull otherwise."

I fetched up against the closed valve at the end of the shaft with a bone-jarring crash that stunned me momentarily. The armor took the impact on the life-support casing at the back of my neck, and I caught the faintest odor of ozone in my breathing air. I didn't report it, but Ariane caught it on the telemetry immediately.

"Kier! Something has short-circuited your oxygen demand metering system. The flow has dropped by 30 percent."

Those were deadly words to me. I didn't know how long I could last in the armor with only 70 percent flow. I could quickly become euphoric from anoxemia, and death wouldn't be far behind. To my own credit, let it be said I was more concerned with how I could inactivate the starship than I was with how long I might last. I turned on my suit lights and saw that I was standing spraddle-legged once again before the almost invisible valve bearing the First Empire symbols that said: *Touch*. It was a familiar thing, and oddly, the familiarity brought a certain crazy comfort. No matter how desperate the situation, I *had* been here before, and I *had* returned to the world of the living. It was *possible*.

I placed my gloved hand on the sensitive pressure latch, and the valve obediently dilated, disclosing the featureless room where Marissa Tran Wyeth had lain in the crystal capsule.

Now I could see again, as I had on the first occasion, that the walls were bare. I E-phoned back to Ariane. "Is Marissa on the circuit?" I asked, trying to seem calm and competent.

"I am here." Marissa's impulses came clearly through the contacts. "Look on the deck under the latches that held the capsule."

I was standing on them. I knelt and discovered a small grid.

"It extrudes if you apply pressure," Marissa said. "But it is a simple vibratory speaker. It won't function properly unless the chamber is pressurized."

There were no other controls—nothing to control an airflow into the room.

"Close the valve," she said.

I went to the wall and touched the reverse side of the

latch. The valve closed obediently. Then I watched the external pressure sensors of my armor. Nothing. I reported back to Ariane and Marissa. Immediately, I felt a surge of apprehension from the girl. Even through the E-phone the Magellanic Mutation projected her emotional responses. "What is it?" I asked.

"The pressurization should have been automatic," she said.

"Is there a manual override?"

"No," she said heavily. "There is not."

I stood in baffled thought. "Maybe the grid will transmit well enough by contact with my armor."

"Try it," Ariane suggested.

"Are we moving?" I asked.

"Yes. Into a low orbit around Sirius Fifteen."

"How low?"

"I haven't been able to compute it. But it looks like about six hundred kilometers."

Marissa said, "The *Death* will make a planetary attack with its secondary weapons and then go on to the star. It isn't functioning rationally."

I had a fleeting impulse to say that none of this was rational, that revenge on this scale was monstrous insanity, that the people of the communes of Magellan must have been raving maniacs ever to conceive such a plan—and then I thought more calmly and accepted what *was*. Snarling and snapping at Marissa would solve no problems.

I extracted the grid from its housing and held it against my helmet. I heard something, but very faintly. It sounded like a distant, distant voice speaking in a foreign language. It was Anglic, I supposed, the language of the First Empire. But I couldn't understand it or even make it out.

"Put the grid next to the E-phone pack," Ariane said. "Maybe I can amplify it."

"Let Marissa translate for me," I said, doing as the cyborg instructed.

I stood for what seemed a long time in that silent place, with the bulkhead walls lit only by my suit lights that cast strange shadows around me. I felt like a man deep in a dungeon cell. I must have experienced a kind of racial memory, reverting emotionally back to the time when my ancestors had fought on horseback and, losing some forgotten battle, found themselves deep in the hold of some prison starship or the stone *oubliettes* of some grim stone castle by a dark and restless sea. It was a sobering experience.

Presently, Ariane said, "The instructions to the Watcher are as follows, Kier: *'Now set all in order with your commands through this grid. Be certain that the* Death *will obey. And when that is done, compose yourself for an honored rest.'*" Her despair was now so clear that it was frightening.

The girl knew something vital. I was sure of it. "Marissa," I said. "What else?"

"The instructions also say—" Her impulses faltered, and I felt my heart sinking. "They also say that the chamber is locked. The valve will not open now."

Long ago, in the Dawn Age, when men had fought their wars with simple machines that sailed the sea and flew in the air, a nation had created something called the Corps of the Divine Wind—pilots who locked themselves in their craft and died with them willingly, to serve their nation. The planners of the communes of Magellan had done the same with the Watchers. I was trapped in the black starship.

Perhaps it was the euphoria induced by a failing oxygen supply, but the notion seemed supremely simple and logical. What else was there for a Watcher? Marissa had told me that they were expected to awaken, check over the instructions, and repair whatever needed to be repaired, and die. The fusing shut of the valve was simply a logical precaution against the possibility that the Watcher, no matter how well indoctrinated, might change his or her mind and opt for life—thus imperiling the mission of the starship built at such great effort.

I looked about me at the *Death*—at *my* death—and grinned foolishly. Of course. Simple, perfect logic. No temptations. What a clever animal was man!

Ariane said sharply, "Kier!" When she had my attention, she said more gently. "The nitrogen count in your blood is rising. That is why you feel as you do." She didn't wait for a reply, which would have been only the expression of an intoxicated man in any case. I was deep in the zone of nitrogen narcosis. It was like drink. "Kier, are you paying attention? Hear me. You have a cutter in your armor. You can cut through the bulkhead."

Not so, I thought vaguely. The cutter was small, the bulkhead thick and hard. It would take time, an eternity of time—

I forced myself to think. Why had I come here? There had to be a reason. I could feel the silly smile on my lips. What was it I came to do? Oh, yes, I had to make the ship stop what it was doing— And what was that? Something bad, something very bad...

"Ariane, Ari—" I called. "Where are we now?"

"Seven hundred kilometers above S-Fifteen. Kier, listen—"

I laughed out loud. It was really so very simple. Once one was relieved of the necessity for self-preservation, everything became more—how should I put it?—*reasonable*. Yes, that was it.

"Ari," I said. "Tell Marissa to give me the right words—the words this foolish monster understands. How do I tell it to turn around? To reverse attitude?"

"What are you planning, Kier?" Ariane asked.

I felt a slight shortness of breath, and my lightheadedness seemed to increase. "Now, Ari. You are *not* Lady Nora. Remember that, now, you simply are *not,* so don't question me about the obvious." I had never spoken so to the cyborg, but it was something I'd often longed to say in my hagridden moments. "I am old enough to make my own decisions, and the first thing I have decided is that this beast must turn about and slow down."

Marissa said, "Kier, use the cutting touch on the valve—please. *Do it now.*"

I heard Ariane talking to Lord Ouspensky aboard the

Intrepid. Was she begging him to make an attack? No, surely not that. The *Death* would do to the battleship what it had done to the Nav cruiser.

"Marissa," I said, growing suddenly very angry, "I need the words, the Anglic words. Stop wasting time."

She gave them to me, and I repeated them to myself, giggling at my atrocious accent. When I had committed them to memory, I held the grid tightly against the face plate of my helmet and shouted them over and over again.

There was a slight inertial change. I could feel it, and it filled me with a gleeful sense of power. The *Death* was following my commands—slowly and incompletely, but it was moving in response to my instructions. For the first time in ten millennia, the great black starship was directly under the command of a human being.

"Tell the *Intrepid* to stay clear, Ariane!" I said exultantly. "The SW forces are in charge here!" I was tempted to break into the song of the SW wings, but I couldn't remember the words.

"Yes, Starkahn," Ariane said. "You are in command."

"Kier!" Marissa interrupted. "I beg you! Start cutting the valve!"

"In time, all in good time." I felt assured and completely in control of the situation. I felt like dancing and laughing, except that it was really very difficult to breathe. I wondered why that was. Ariane would know. I would ask her, just as soon as I got the next evolution under way.

"What is the starship doing now, Ari?" I asked.

"It has reversed attitude, Starkahn."

"Now, Marissa. I want it to retrothrust enough to decay the orbit on this revolution," I said. "Can you translate the instructions for that?"

"I—I—don't know, Kier," the girl said.

"Have Ariane compute the amount of thrust. Come along, girl. We haven't all the time there is, you know." In fact, I thought with a touch of maudlin sentiment, *We haven't much time at all. Poor Lady Nora—she was going to be terribly upset about this. She would probably be angry with*

Ariane,too. No more Starkahn. No more happy Royalist plots. No more son Kier—

Marissa's message came through the E-phone. I gave the order to retrofire, to slow orbital speed to the velocity of destruction in the heat of atmospheric entry.

I felt Ariane say, presumably to Marissa, though I couldn't be certain: "Will the ship make an attack as it touches the atmosphere?"

"I don't know," Marissa replied. I received another surge of emotional empathy from the girl through the encephalophone contacts. She was weeping. For me, I wondered? That was remarkable. Was this thing she was feeling—love? *How marvelous*, I thought. *And how sad, because now there was almost no time left, no time at all.*

I shouted again through the face plate into the grid. For a moment there was no response because even the damaged positronic brain of the great ship, primitive as it was, realized it was an order that would result in self-destruction.

Then, like a true robot, it responded. The cores released a burst of energy against the direction of motion. I was slammed hard against the wall of the compartment by the swiftly mounting G-force. The dazing impact half sobered me, and I had a clear and lucid moment during which I knew what was happening to me.

All my defenses crumbled, and the age-old curse of man— his fear of death—came pouring through. My oxygen-starved brain reeled under the blow. And in that moment—

—I was Erit, I was Marissa. Somehow, I was Ariane, too, because I could see everything. I saw the night of space, and bright Sirius, and below me I saw the mottled blue and green and white planet covered by a restless sea. In the distance I could make out the slender shapes of the Fleet warships standing helplessly by, and I could see the Death, *as well, as Ariane saw it: a pattern of electrical impulses and atomic movements beautiful beyond compare; and as Erit saw it: a shape of radiances, pseudo life-forces in the cubic miles of nucleonic circuitry with my own human aura deeply centered in the sparkling, living mass; and as Mar-*

*issa saw it: a darkness falling, like a dark meteoroid toward
the first wisps of the planet's upper air. I saw all of that at
once and intermingled with the walls and the shape and the
textures of the tiny compartment that imprisoned me.*

*I understood—everything that was happening. I even
understood how it happened and what a marvel it was. The
moment of great stress and anger had created a new thing
in the galaxy. The moment had been midwife to a new kind
of being. Erit the Vulk (and in her-me I sensed the presence
of Gret, the ethos of him intact and immortal) and Marissa
with her Magellanic Mutation that caused an outflowing of
emotional energies, and Ariane with her marvelous cyborg
powers had all combined in a near-miraculous Triad. And
because I was the cause of it, because it was their concern
and love for me that fused them together, they—together—
reached out across the intervening space to the black starship—to me—and formed this new quadripartite being:
four dissimilar creatures sharing their essence and their
knowledge ... and their powers.*

We agreed that this stellar being must not die with the
Death.

And as the starship began to glow with the first heat of
friction in S-Fifteen's atmosphere (I could see it happening
in three modes), I flung myself at the valve, cutter in hand,
and began to work.

The laser cut with agonizing slowness, and there was
already heat in the walls from the starship's steepening fall.
I didn't need to be told what was happening. I was aware
of it as I have been aware of nothing before in my life. I
could literally see the atomic structure of the metal changing
under the laser. I could see the starship falling, beginning
to tumble now out of control, a vast planetoid of metal
rolling end for end through S-Fifteen's stratosphere. I could
understand the vessel's weaponry and neutralize it easily
now, but none of that mattered because the last *Death* was
falling inexorably into the Sirian Sea.

The oxygen flow from my life-support pack was very

low, but I was cyborg enough to simulate Ariane's ability to oxidize from my own bodily resources. It would not last long, but for the moment I *was* a cyborg. I was Marissa, too, *wanting* most desperately to live and be part of this new thing that we had all created. And I was Erit, calm and wise with the wisdom of understanding and near immortality. I worked swiftly and without fear.

Still I fell, entombed in cubic kilometers of metal, toward the cobalt sea. I could feel the threat of the danger, yet I could sense the placid beauty of the deep ocean toward which I fell, now streaming fire as the surface of the starship glowed white.

We were all together in that compartment: Erit, Ariane, Marissa, and I. And the laser cut steadily through the metal, a tiny bubbling trail of bright slag that formed globules and floated free in zero-gravity each time the massive vessel changed direction.

The heat was making the paintwork smoulder when the valve was free at last. I computed the distance from the surface of the sea and the speed of my fall. There was barely time. I jetted through the jagged opening and up the now blazing-hot shaft.

When I neared the opening, I was in flames. The heat was burbling through the opening, blue-green. I caught a glimpse of the sea through the fire. The hatchway was pointed down. I went through without hesitation, out into the blazing, streaming open air. The noise was deafening, and the impact of the air was like the crash of a hundred hammers. I felt my armor twist and scorch, and I fell free, trailing the metal drogues, watching them flutter and snap and finally burn away.

Below me there was a cataclysmic tower of steam and flaming fragments as the disintegrating starship struck the sea. The superheated water erupted into a mushroom-shaped flower as the shock wave hit it; then the sea parted into an immense watery crater to swallow the *Death* in one single, convulsive gulp, and in the next instant the sea rushed in again to rise into another tower of steam and fire even greater than before. I was on the edges of it, and I was born aloft, tumbled like a leaf in a wind, and all around me black storm clouds formed instantly as the tortured air tried to cool the violence of the explosion.

Then I was falling again, riding my crippled thrusters, spinning back toward the ocean that was suddenly dark, almost black, with the churned-up debris of a bottom five kilometers below the sunlighted surface.

I struck the sea and arrowed into the murky depths. I could feel the heat of the water through the armor. I went deeper and deeper still, tumbled by turbulent currents, and gradually the violent movements of the water around me became calmer, for even the mightiest violence of man cannot perturb the seas of the universe for long.

At long last I was floating in clear, dark blue water. The weight of my useless armor was carrying me down, down.

I remembered (or was it one of the others of me who remembered?) the implant still in my chest: the gill put there when I was a pleasure-seeker of Zodiac Bay. I opened my space armor and let the warm waters of the sea float me free. It was peaceful in the depths, dark and peaceful as the night of space between the galaxies. I could remember that, too, for I was Marissa as well as the others.

Then with a deep draft of cooling water in my gill, I started upward toward the light, toward the sparkling surface where I could see, even at this distance, the lovely winged shape of Ariane waiting for me to return.

Epilogue

*The heavens declare the glory of God; and the fir-
mament showeth his handiwork.*

> Psalm, attributed to David,
> period unknown

THIS manuscript, done in the ancient style of my human
forebears, is being dispatched on our last drone. We are far
from Rhada, far from the Rim. The last star king has left
the land of my fathers.

It is possible the Galacton would not voluntarily have
given us permission to depart on this search, for he is, above
all else, a practical man, and he sees no immediate advantage to this journey. We used our developing mental powers
on him, and he agreed. It is best that we go, for we are no
longer simply a man, a woman, a Vulk, and a cyborg. We
are one entity that is all four, with capabilities that we can

165

only imagine now, for we are still young. But though we love our fellow creatures, there is no longer a place for us among the worlds of men.

At this moment we are traveling at four kilolights, and even at this speed our journey will be very long. But with the strength and speed of Ariane, with the wisdom and long life of Vulk Erit, and the love and community of the Cloud-woman our common property—what else were we to do?

Ahead of us lies the Cloud. And beyond?

We—shall—see.

MORE *SCIENCE* *FICTION* *ADVENTURE!*